P9-AFQ-534

THE DEMON PRINCES

It may well be asked how, from so many thieves, kidnappers, pirates, slavers, and assassins, one can isolate five individuals and identify them as "Demon Princes." The author can define the criteria that establish the Five as arch-fiends and overlords of evil.

First: The Demon Princes are typified by grandeur.

Second: these men are constructive geniuses, motivated not by malice, perversity, greed, or misanthropy, but by violent inner purposes, which are for the most part shrouded and obscure.

Third: each of the Demon Princes is a mystery; each insists on anonymity and facelessness.

Fourth: and obverse to the aforementioned, is a quality best to be described as absolute pride, absolute self-sufficiency.

Fifth: and ample in itself, I cite the historic conclave of 1500 at Smade's Tavern where the five acknowledged themselves as peers and defined their various areas of interest.

—From Introduction to *The Demon Princes* (Elucidarian Press, Vega.)

THE
KILLING
MACHINE

Jack Vance

DAW BOOKS, INC.
DONALD A. WOLLHEIM, PUBLISHER
1633 Broadway, New York, NY 10019

Copyright ©, 1964, by Jack Vance.

All Rights Reserved.

Cover art by Gino D'Achille.

First DAW printing, october 1978

4 5 6 7 8 9

PRINTED IN U.S.A.

CHAPTER 1

From "How the Planets Trade," by Ignace Wodlecki: *Cosmopolis*, September, 1509:

In all commercial communities, the prevalence or absence of counterfeit money, spurious bills of exchange, forged notes-of-hand, or any of a dozen other artifices to augment the value of blank paper is a matter of great concern. Across the Oikumene, precise duplication and reproducing machines are readily available; and only meticulous safeguards preclude the chronic debasement of our currency. These safeguards are three: first, the single negotiable currency is the Standard Value Unit, or SVU, notes for which, in various denominations, are issued only by the Bank of Sol, the Bank of Rigel, and the Bank of Vega. Second, each genuine note is characterized by a 'quality of authenticity.' Third, the three banks make widely available the so-called fakemeter. This is a pocket device that, when a counterfeit note is passed through a slot, sounds a warning buzzer. As all small boys know, attempts to disassemble the fake-meter are futile; as soon as the case is damaged, it destroys itself.

Regarding the 'quality of authenticity' there is naturally a good deal of speculation. Apparently in certain key areas, a particular molecular configuration is introduced, resulting in a standard reactance of some nature: electrical capacity? magnetic permeability? photo-absorption or reflectance? isotopic variation? radioactive doping? a combination of some or all of these qualities? Only a handful of persons know and they won't tell.

Gersen first encountered Kokor Hekkus at the age of nine. Crouching behind an old barge, he watched slaughter, pillage, enslavement. This was the historic Mount Pleasant Massacre, notable for the unprecedented cooperation of the five so-called Demon Princes. Kirth Gersen and his grandfather survived; five names became as familiar to Gersen as his own: Attel Malagate, Viole Falushe, Lens Larque, Howard Alan

Treesong, Kokor Hekkus. Each had his distinctive quality. Malagate was insensate and grim, Viole Falushe gloried in sybaritical refinements, Lens Larque was a megalomaniac, Howard Alan Treesong a chaoticist. Kokor Hekkus was the most mercurial, fantastic, and inaccessible, the most daring and inventive. A few folk had reported their impressions: uniformly they found him affable, restless, unpredictable, and infected with what might have seemed utter madness, except for his demonstrable control and strength. As to his appearance, all had different opinions. He was, by popular repute, immortal.

Gersen's second encounter with Kokor Hekkus occurred in the course of a routine mission Beyond, and was indecisive—or so it seemed at the time. In early April of 1525, Ben Zaum, an official of the IPCC,* arranged a clandestine interview with Gersen and proposed a stint of "weaseling"—that is to say, an IPCC investigation Beyond. Gersen's own affairs had come to a standstill: he was bored and restless, and so agreed at least to listen to the proposition.

The job, as Zaum explained it, was simplicity itself. The IPCC had been commissioned to locate a certain fugitive: "Call him 'Mr. Hoskins,'" said Zaum. So urgently required was Mr. Hoskins that at least thirty operatives were being despatched to various sectors of the Beyond. Gersen's job would be to survey the inhabited localities of a certain planet: "Call it 'Bad World,'" said Zaum, with a knowing grin. Gersen must either locate Mr. Hoskins or establish as a definite certainty that he had not set foot on Bad World.

Gersen reflected a moment. Zaum, who reveled in mystification, on this occasion seemed to be outdoing himself. Patiently Gersen began to chip away at the exposed part of the iceberg, hoping to float new areas into view. "Why only thirty weasels? To do the job right, you'd need a thousand."

Zaum's wise expression gave him the semblance of a large blond owl. "We've been able to narrow the area of search. I can say this much, Bad World is one of the likelier spots—which is why I want you to take it on. I can't overemphasize how important all this is."

Gersen decided he didn't want the job. Zaum had deter-

---

* IPCC—Interworld Police Coordination Company: in theory, a private organization providing the police systems of the Oikumene specialized consultation, a central information file, criminological laboratories; in practice; a supergovernmental agency occasionally functioning as a law in itself.

mined—or was under orders—to maintain as much reticence as possible. Working in the dark irritated Gersen, distracted him, and so reduced his effectiveness—which meant that he might not return from the Beyond. Gersen wondered how to turn down the job without alienating Ben Zaum and so drying up a pipeline into the IPCC. "What if I found Mr. Hoskins?" he asked.

"You have four options, which I'll name in order of decreasing desirability. Bring him to Alphanor alive. Bring him to Alphanor dead. Infect him with one of your horrible Sarkoy mind-drugs. Kill him outright."

"I'm no assassin."

"This is more than simple assassination! This is—confound it, I'm not permitted to explain in detail. But it's truly urgent, I assure you of this!"

"I don't disbelieve you," said Gersen. "Still, I won't—in fact, I can't—kill without knowing why. You'd better get someone else."

Under normal circumstances, Zaum would have terminated the interview, but he persisted. Gersen thereby was given to understand that either qualified weasels were hard to come by or that Zaum regarded his services highly.

"If money is any object," said Zaum, "I think I can arrange—"

"I think I'll pass this one up."

Zaum made a half-serious display of beating his forehead with his fists. "Gersen—you're one of the few men whose competence I'm sure of. This is a murderously delicate operation—if, of course, Mr. Hoskins visits Bad World, which I myself think is likely. I'll tell you this much: Kokor Hekkus is involved. If he and this Mr. Hoskins make contact—" he flung up his hands.

Gersen maintained his attitude of disinterest, but now all was changed. "Is Mr. Hoskins a criminal?"

Zaum's bland brow creased in discomfiture. "I can't go into details."

"In that case, how do you expect me to identify him?"

"You'll get photographs and physical characteristics; this should suffice. The job is perfectly simple. Find the man: kill him, confuse him, or bring him back to Alphanor."

Gersen shrugged. "Very well. But since I'm indispensable I want more money."

Zaum made a peevish complaint or two. "Now as to definite arrangements: when can you leave?"

"Tomorrow."

"You still keep your spacecraft?"

"If you call the Model 9B Locator a spacecraft."

"It gets you there and back, and it's suitably inconspicuous. Where is it docked?"

"At Avente Spaceport, Area C, Bay 10."

Zaum made a note. "Tomorrow go to your spaceship, make departure. The ship will be provisioned and fueled. The monitor will be coded to Bad World. You will find a folder with information regarding Mr. Hoskins in your *Star Directory*. You need only personal effects—weapons and the like.

"How long am I to search Bad World?"

Zaum heaved a deep sigh. "I wish I could tell you. I wish I knew what was going on. . . . If you don't find him within a month after arrival, it's probably too late. If we only knew for sure where he was going, what were his motivations. . . ."

"I gather he's not a known criminal then."

"No. He's lived a long, useful life. Then he was approached by a man named Seuman Otwal, who we suspect to be an agent of Kokor Hekkus. Mr. Hoskins, according to his wife, thereupon seemed to go to pieces."

"Extortion? Blackmail?"

"In these circumstances—impossible."

Gersen was able to elicit no more information.

Arriving at Avente Spaceport somewhat before noon of the following day, Gersen found matters as Zaum had stated. Boarding the spartan little spacecraft, he went first to the *Star Directory*, where he found a manila envelope containing photographs, plus a printed description. Mr. Hoskins was shown in various costumes, headgear, and skin-toning. He appeared a man in his late maturity, with a big loose body, affable large eyes, a wide mouth with heavy teeth, a small rapacious nose. Mr. Hoskins was an Earthman: so much was clear from his clothes and skin-toning, which were generally similar but different in detail to those of Alphanor. Gersen put the folder aside, reluctantly decided against a visit to Earth, where he probably could identify Mr. Hoskins. Such a detour would take too much time—and undoubtedly get him into the IPCC's blackbook. He made a final check of the boat, called Port Control for departure processing.

Half an hour later, Alphanor was a shining orb astern. Gersen engaged the monitor, and watched as the nose of the boat swept across the sky, finally to point in a direction sixty degrees off the baseline between Rigel and Sol.

The Jarnell Coverdrive now seized the ship, or, more accurately, created conditions where a few pounds of thrust caused near-insantaneity of transfer.

Time passed. Random photons curling and seeping through the Jarnell laminae entered the ship, to allow the outside universe to be seen: stars by the hundreds and thousands, drifting past like sparks on the wind. Gersen kept a careful astrogational record, fixing on Sol, Canopus, and Rigel. Presently the ship crossed the separation between the Oikumene and the Beyond, and now law, order, civilization, had no formal existence. Projecting the line of travel, Gersen finally was able to identify Bad World: Carina LO-461 IV in the *Star Directory*, Bissom's End in the terminology of Beyond. Henry Bissom was seven-hundred-years dead; the world, or at least the region surrounding the principal town Skouse, was now the preserve of the Windle family. Bad World was no misnomer, thought Gersen; in fact, should he put down at Skouse without good reason—offhand he could think of none—he would without fail be picked up by the local platoon of the Deweaseling Corp.* He would be rigorously questioned. After which, if he were lucky, he would be allowed ten minutes to leave the planet. If weaseling were suspected, he would be killed. Gersen thought harsh thoughts concerning Ben Zaum and his overelaborate secrecy. Had he known his destination, he might conceivably have set up some kind of cover.

Ahead a greenish-yellow star of no great luminosity clung to the crosshairs, waxing brighter and larger. Presently the intersplit kicked off; ether collapsing in upon the ship sighed and shuddered through all the atoms of ship and Gersen himself: a sound to set the teeth on edge, but which perhaps wasn't even real.

The old Model 9B coasted through space. Nearby hung Bissom's End—Bad World. It was a smallish planet, cold at the poles, with a chain of low mountains forming a cincture of the equator, like a weld joining the two hemispheres. To north and south ran belts of sea, shallowing somewhat near 50 degrees latitude to bayous and jungles, beyond which were swamps and morasses all the way to the permafrost.

On a windy plateau sat the town Skouse, an irregular huddle of dingy stone buildings. Gersen was puzzled. Why would Mr. Hoskins want to come to Bissom's End? Far more

* The single interworld organization of Beyond, existing only to identify and destroy undercover agents of the IPCC.

pleasant refuges existed. Brinktown was almost gay. . . . But he was taking too much for granted: Mr. Hoskins might never come near Bissom's End, with the whole mission a mare's nest; indeed, Zaum had emphasized as much.

Gersen examined the planet under the macroscope, finding little of interest. The equatorial mountains were dusty and barren, the oceans were gray and mottled with the shadows of low scudding clouds. He turned his attention back to Skouse, a town of perhaps three or four thousand population. Nearby was a scorched field bordered by sheds and warehouses: evidently the spaceport. Nowhere were luxurious mansions or castles to be seen, and Gersen remembered that the Windles inhabited caves in the mountains behind the town. A hundred miles to east and west, evidences of habitation finally dwindled to wilderness. There was a single other town, beside a dock extending into the North Ocean. Nearby was a metal-processing plant, so Gersen deduced from slag tailings and several large buildings. Elsewhere the planet showed no signs of human occupation.

If he could not visit Skouse overtly, he must do so surreptitiously. He picked out an isolated ravine, waited till evening shadows crossed the area, then settled as swiftly as possible.

He spent an hour adjusting to the atmosphere, then stepped out into the night. The air was cool; like that of almost every planet it had a distinctive tang, to which the nostrils quickly become dulled: in this case a bitter chemical exhalation mixed with something like burnt spice, the one apparently derived from the soil, the other from the native vegetation.

Gersen invested himself with various tools of the weasel trade, winched down his platform flyer, set forth to the west.

The first night Gersen reconnoitered Skouse. The streets were unpaved and aimless; there was a commissary, several warehouses, a garage, three churches, two temples, and a tramway with spindly tracks leading down toward the ocean. He located the inn: a square three-story structure built of stone, fiber panels, and timber. Skouse was a dull town, exuding a sense of boredom, sluggishness, and ignorance; Gersen assumed the population to have little more status than serfdom.

He concentrated his attention on the inn, where Mr. Hoskins, if he were present, would almost certainly take up residence. He was unable to find a window to look through; the stone walls resisted his eavesdrop microphone. And he dared not speak to any of the patrons who at various times during the night staggered out and away through the twisting streets of Skouse.

The second night he had no better success. However, across from the inn, he found a vacated structure: apparently at one time a machine-shop or fabricating plant, but now given over to dust and small white insects unnervingly like minuscule monkeys. Here Gersen ensconced himself and through the entirety of the greenish-yellow day kept watch upon the inn. The life of the town moved past him; dour men and stolid women wearing dark jackets, loose flapping trousers of brown or maroon, black hats with upturned brims, went about their affairs. They spoke in a broad flat dialect that Gersen could never hope to imitate; so died a tentative plan to secure native-style garments and enter the inn. In the late afternoon, strangers came into town: spacemen by their costumes, from a ship that apparently had only just landed. Gersen fought off drowsiness with an antisleep pill. As soon as the sun descended, bringing a mud-colored twilight, he left his hiding place and hurried through the dim streets to the spaceport. Sure enough, a large cargo-ship had put in and was now discharging bales and crates from its hold. Even as Gersen watched, three members of the crew left the ship, crossed the floodlit fore-area, showed passes to the guard at the wicket, and turned down the road toward town.

Gersen joined them. He gave them "Good evening," which they returned with civility, and inquired the name of their ship.

"The *Ivan Garfang*," he was told, "out of Chalcedon."

"Chalcedon, Earth?"

"The same."

The youngest of the group asked, "What kind of a town is Skouse? Any fun to be had?"

"None," said Gersen. "There's an inn, and very little else. It's a dull town and I'm anxious to depart. Are you carrying passengers?"

"Aye, we've one aboard, and room for four more. Five, should Mr. Hosey disembark, as I believe is his plan. Though for what purpose he comes here—" the youth shook his head in incomprehension.

So, thought Gersen, it was to be as easy as that. Who could Mr. Hosey be but Mr. Hoskins? And now, where did Kokor Hekkus fit into the picture? He led the three spacemen to the inn and entered with them, by all appearances their shipmate and, so, secure against deweaseler suspicion.

Gersen cemented the association by calling for a round of

drinks. There was nothing to be had but beer, which was thin and sour, and a white pungent arrack.

The interior of the inn was cheerful enough, with the traditional bar, and fire blazing in the fireplace. A barmaid wearing a limp red smock and straw slippers served the drinks. The youngest of the spacemen, who called himself Carlo, made overtures, to which the maid responded with a look of uncomprehending confusion.

"Leave her alone," advised the oldest of the spacemen whose name was Bude. "She's not all there." He tapped his forehead significantly.

"All the way we come, to the back of Beyond," grumbled Carlo, "and the first woman we spy is a half-wit."

"Leave her for Mr. Hosey," suggested Halvy, the remaining spaceman. "If he disembarks, he'll have a long, dull time of it."

"Some sort of scientist?" asked Gersen. "Or a journalist? They sometimes choose to visit odd places."

"Devil knows what he is," said Carlo. "He hasn't spoken more than two words the entire trip."

The conversation changed. Gersen would have liked to talk more of Mr. Hosey, but dared not ask questions, which Beyond almost always implied a sinister aftermath.

A number of locals had entered the inn, and stood before the fire drinking pints of beer at a gulp, and talking in their flat voices. Gersen took the bartender aside and inquired regarding accommodation.

The bartender shook his head. "It's been so long since we've housed anyone that our beds are all stale. You'll do better back on your ship."

Gersen looked across the room to Carlo, Bude, and Halvy. They showed no disposition for imminent departure. He turned back to the bartender. "Is there someone to run an errand to the ship for me?"

"There's a boy in the back who might oblige."

"I'll speak to him."

The boy was duly summoned: a blank-faced youth, the son of the bartender. Gersen tipped him liberally and made him repeat three times the message he wished delivered. "I'm to ask for Mr. Hosey and say he's wanted at the inn immediately."

"Correct. Be quick now, and there may be more money for you. Remember, give the message to none but Mr. Hosey himself."

The boy departed. Gersen waited a moment, then sauntered from the inn, and followed the boy to the spaceport, keeping well to the rear.

The boy was known to the guard at the spaceport, and after a word or two was allowed onto the field. Gersen approached as close as he dared, and standing in the shadow of a tall bush watched and waited.

Several minutes passed. The boy emerged from the ship—alone. Gersen grunted in disappointment. When the boy came out into the road, Gersen accosted him. Startled, the boy yelped and sprang away.

"Come back here," said Gersen. "Did you see Mr. Hosey?"

"Yes sir, so I did."

Gersen brought out a photograph of Mr. Hoskins, flashed a light. "This gentleman here?"

The boy squinted. "Yes sir. The very same."

"And what did he say?"

The boy glanced sidewise, whites of his eyes gleaming. "He asked if I knew Billy Windle."

"Billy Windle, eh?"

"Yes sir. And of course I don't. Billy Windle's a hormagaunt. He said to tell you, if you were Billy Windle, to come to the ship. I said no, you were a spaceman. And he said he'd deal with none but Billy Windle himself and in person."

"I see. And what's a hormagaunt?"

"That's what we call them here. Maybe on your world you've a different name. They're the folk who soak up other folk's lives and then go off to live on Thamber."

"Billy Windle lives on Thamber?"

The boy nodded earnestly. "It's a real world, never think different. I know, because the hormagaunts live there."

Gersen smiled. "As well as dragons and fairies and ogres and linderlings."

The boy said dolefully, "You don't believe me."

Gersen brought forth more money. "Return to Mr. Hosey. Tell him that Billy Windle waits for him in the road, and bring him out here to me."

The boy's eyes rolled in awe. "Are you Billy Windle?"

"Never mind who I am. Go give Mr. Hosey the message."

The boy returned to the ship. Five minutes later, he came down the gangramp followed by Mr. Hosey—who was quite definitely Mr. Hoskins. They set forth across the field.

But now floating down through the dark sky came a whirling disk of red and blue lights, which swooped and settled to the ground. It was a sumptuous flying car, decorated in the most elaborate fashion, with colored lumes, golden scrolls, and fluttering fronds of green and gold. The rider was a slim, long-legged man with muscular shoulders, as flamboyantly dressed as his boat. His face was tinted black-brown; his features were flexible, regular, youthful; he wore a tight turban of white cloth with a pair of roguish tassels hanging by his right ear. He was charged with nervous vitality; jumping to the ground, he seemed to bounce.

The boy and Mr. Hoskins had halted; the newcomer walked swiftly across the field. He spoke to Mr. Hoskins, who seemed surprised and gestured questioningly toward the road. This must be Billy Windle, thought Gersen, gritting his teeth in frustration. Billy Windle glanced toward the road, then made an inquiry of Mr. Hoskins, who reluctantly seemed to assent, and tapped his pouch. But in the same motion he produced a weapon, which he displayed to Billy Windle in a nervous truculent fashion, as if to emphasize that he trusted no one. Billy Windle merely laughed.

Where did Kokor Hekkus enter the picture? Was Billy Windle one of his agents? There was a simple and direct way to find out. The guard at the gate was watching the confrontation with fascinated attention. He did not hear Gersen come up behind him; he felt nothing as Gersen struck him a deft blow, which instantly induced unconsciousness. Gersen donned the guard's cap and cape, marched officiously toward Billy Windle and Mr. Hoskins. They were engaged in a transfer: each held an envelope. Billy Windle glanced toward Gersen, waved him back toward the gate, but Gersen continued to approach, trying to appear obsequious. "Back to your post, guard," snapped Billy Windle. "Leave us to our affairs." There was something inexpressibly dire in the poise of his head.

"Pardon me, sir," said Gersen. He jumped forward, clubbed at Billy Windle's gorgeous headgear with his projac. As Billy Windle staggered and fell, Gersen raked Mr. Hoskins' arm with a low-charge jolt, jarring loose his weapon.

Mr. Hoskins cried out in pain and astonishment. Gersen scooped up Billy Windle's envelope, reached for that which Mr. Hoskins held. Mr. Hoskins staggered back, then as Gersen rasied his projac, halted.

Gersen shoved him toward Billy Windle's air-car. "Quick. Get aboard. Or I'll punish you."

Mr. Hoskins' legs were rubbery; lurching and tottering, he moved at a shambling trot to the air-car. As he climbed aboard, he tried to stuff the envelope into his shirt; Gersen reached, snatched; the envelope tore; there was a brief struggle and Gersen held half the envelope, with the other half somewhere on the ground under the boat. Billy Windle was staggering to his feet. Gersen could delay no longer. The air-car controls were standard; he thrust the lift-arm far across. Billy Windle shouted something Gersen could not hear, then, as the air-car slanted up, brought forth his projac, fired. The bolt sang past Gersen's ear, cut diagonally across Mr. Hoskins' head. Gersen fired back as the air-car swung across the sky, but the range was long and he merely kicked up a blaze of lambent dust.

High above Skouse, he swerved, flew west, settled beside his spaceboat. He carried the corpse of Mr. Hoskins aboard, and abandoning the bedizened air-car, took the Model 9B into space. He engaged the intersplit and now was safe: no known human effort could intercept him. Mission accomplished in a workmanlike fashion, without undue exertion: Mr. Hoskins killed and en route to Alphanor, as per instructions. In short, sheer routine. Gersen should have been pleased, but this was not the case. He had learned nothing, succeeded with nothing; nothing except the paltry business for which he had been sent to Bissom's End. Kokor Hekkus had been involved in the affair; with Mr. Hoskins dead, Gersen would never know why or how.

The corpse was a problem. Gersen dragged it into the rear locker, shut the door on it.

He brought forth the envelope he had taken from billy Windle, opened it. Within was a sheet of pink paper on which someone had written in florid purple ink. The message was tilted: *How to become a hormagaunt.* Gersen raised his eyebrows: jest? Somehow he did not think so. Gersen read the instructions with a small *frisson* of horror tickling at his neck. They were unpleasant.

  Aging is pursuivant to a condition in which the ichors of youth have been exhausted: so much is inherently obvious. The hormagaunt will desire to replenish himself with these invaluable elixirs from the most obvious source: the persons of those who are young. The process is expensive unless one has access to a sufficient number of such persons, and in this case he proceeds in the following fashion:

Instructions followed:

From the bodies of living children, the hormagaunt must procure certain glands and organs, prepare extracts, from which a waxy nodule might ultimately be derived. This nodule implanted in the hormagaunt's pineal gland forfends age.

Gersen put the letter aside, and inspected the fragment he had wrenched from Mr. Hoskins. It read:

—crimps, or more properly, bands of density. These apparently occur at random, though in practice they are so casual as to be imperceptible. The critical spacing is in terms of the square root of the first eleven primes. The occurrence of six or more such crimps at any of the designated locations will validate—

Gersen found the reference incomprehensible, but vastly intriguing: what had Mr. Hoskins known so valuable that it might be traded on an even basis for the secret of perpetual youth?

He examined again the horrid directions for becoming a hormagaunt, and wondered if they were sound. Then he destroyed both sets of instructions.

At Avente Spaceport, he called Ben Zaum by visiphone. "I'm back."

Zaum rasied his eyebrows. "So soon?"

"There was no reason to delay."

Thirty minutes later Zaum and Gersen met in the vestibule to the spaceport's waiting room. "Where is Mr. Hoskins?" Along with the delicate emphasis on the Hoskins, he gave Gersen a low of narrow inquiry.

"You'll need a hearse. He's been dead for some time. Since before I left Bad World—as you identified it."

"Did he—what were the circumstances?"

"He and a man called Billy Windle had struck some sort of a bargain, but they could not come to terms. Windle seemed very disappointed and killed Mr. Hoskins. I managed to recover the body."

Zaum gave Gersen a glance of mild suspicion. "Did any papers change hands? In other words did Windle derive any information from Hoskins?"

"No."

"You're sure of this?"

"Absolutely."

Zaum was still not completely at ease. "This is all you have to report?"

"Isn't it enough? You have Mr. Hoskins, which is what you wanted."

Zaum licked his lips, glanced at Gersen from the corners of his eyes. "You found no papers on his body?"

"No. And I want to ask you a question."

Zaum heaved a deep dissatisfied sigh. "Very well. If possible, I'll answer."

"You mentioned Kokor Hekkus. How does he come into the matter?"

Zaum deliberated a moment, scratching his chin. "Kokor Hekkus is a man of many identities. One of them is, or so we have been informed, Billy Windle."

Gersen nodded sadly. "I feared as much. . . . I missed my opportunity. It may never come again. . . . Do you know what a hormagaunt is?"

"A what?"

"A hormagaunt. It seems to be an immortal creature who lives on Thamber."

In a measured voice Zaum said, "I don't know what a hormagaunt is and all I know about Thamber is 'set your course by the old Dog Star till faring past the verge extreme, dead ahead shines Thamber's gleam'—however the song goes".

"You forgot the line after 'old Dog Star': 'A point to the north of Achernar.' "

"No matter," said Zaum. "I never found the Land of Oz either." He sighed lugubriously. "I suspect that you're not telling me the whole story. But—"

"But what?"

"Be discreet."

"Oh indeed."

"And be sure that if you thwarted Kokor Hekkus in one of his schemes you will meet him again. He never repays a favor and never forgets a wrong."

CHAPTER 2

From Introduction to *The Demon Princes*, by Caril Carphen (Elucidarian Press, New Wexford, Aloysius, Vega):

It may well be asked how, from so many thieves, kidnapers, pirates, slavers, and assassins within and beyond the Pale, one can isolate five individuals and identify them as 'Demon Princes.' The author, while conceding to a certain degree of arbitrariness, can nevertheless in good conscience define the criteria that in his mind establish the Five as arch-fiends and overlords of evil.

First: the Demon Princes are typified by grandeur. Consider the manner in which Kokor Hekkus gained his cognomen 'The Killing Machine,' or Attel Malagate's 'plantation' on Grabhorne Planet (a civilization of his own definition), or Lens Larque's astounding monument to himself, or Viole Falushe's Palace of Love. Certainly these are not the works of ordinary men, nor the results of ordinary vices (though Viole Falushe is said to be physically vain, and in certain exploits of Kokor Hekkus there is the quaintly horrid quality of a small boy's experiments with an insect).

Second: these men are constructive geniuses, motivated not by malice, perversity, greed, or misanthropy, but by violent inner purposes, which are for the most part shrouded and obscure. Why does Howard Alan Treesong glory in chaos? What are the goals of the inscrutable Attel Malagate, or that fascinating flamboyant Kokor Hekkus?

Third: each of the Demon Princes is a mystery; each insists on anonymity and facelessness. Even to close associates these men are unknown; each is friendless, loveless (we can safely discount the self-indulgences of the sybaritical Viole Falushe).

Fourth: and obverse to the aforementioned, is a quality best to be described as absolute pride, absolute self-sufficiency. Each considers the relationship between himself and the balance of humanity as no more than a confrontation of equals.

Fifth: and ample in itself, I cite the historic conclave of 1500 at Smade's Tavern (to be discussed in Chapter

One) where the five acknowledged themselves, grudgingly perhaps, as peers, and defined their various areas of interest. *Ipsi dixeunt!*

Such was Gersen's second encounter with Kokor Hekkus. The aftermath was a period of depression, during which Gersen spent long mornings and afternoons on the Avente Esplanade, gazing out over the Thaumaturge Ocean. For a period, he had considered a return to Bissom's End—but the project seemed rash and almost certainly pointless: Kokor Hekkus would not stay long at Bissom's End. Gersen must somehow make a new contact.

This was a resolve easier to form than to implement. Hairraising anecdotes by the dozen circulated regarding Kokor Hekkus, but specific information was rare. The reference to Thamber was new, but Gersen gave it small consideration: it could hardly be more than the fantasy of an imaginative boy.

Time passed—a week, two weeks. Kokor Hekkus received mention in the news as the presumptive kidnaper of a Copus, Pi Cassiopeia VIII, mercantilist. Gersen was mildly surprised; the Demon Princes seldom kidnapped for ransom.

Two days later came news of another kidnaping, the scene on this occasion being the Hakluz Mountains of Orpo, Pi Cassiopeia VII; the victim a wealthy packer of sour-spore. Again Kokor Hekkus was reputedly involved: indeed only the possible participation of Kokor Hekkus made the not uncommon crimes noteworthy.

Gersen's third encounter with Kokor Hekkus arose directly, if deviously, as a result of the kidnapings; and indeed the kidnapings themselves followed as a reverse or backhanded consequence to Gersen's success at Skouse.

The chain of events was expedited by chance. One midmorning Gersen sat on a bench halfway along the Esplanade; an elderly man, with the pale blue skin-toning, black jacket, and beige trousers of middle-class gentility, took a seat on the other end of the bench. Some minutes later he muttered an expletive, threw aside his newspaper, and looking toward Gersen expressed indignation in regard to the lawlessness of the times. "Another kidnaping, another innocent person whisked off to Interchange! Why cannot these crimes be halted? What is the constabulary about? They warn persons of means to caution. What a sorry condition!"

Gersen expressed whole-hearted agreement, but said that he knew no effective solution to the problem other than making illegal the private ownership of spacecraft.

"Why not?" demanded the old man. "I possess no spaceship, nor do I feel the need to do so. At best they are instruments of frivolity and ostentation; at worst they facilitate the commission of crime, and especially kidnaping. Look you—" he tapped the newspaper "—ten kidnapings, all made possible by the spaceship!"

"Ten?" asked Gersen in surprise. "So many?"

"Ten in the last two weeks, all persons of extreme wealth and worth. The ransoms go Beyond, to enrich rascals; it is money dissipated in space, a loss to us all!" He went on to remark that moral values had deteriorated since his youth; that respect for law and order had reached an all-time nadir; that only the most inept or unlucky criminal suffered for his acts. To exemplify his convictions, he cited a man he had seen only the day previously, a man whom he recognized as an associate of the notorious Kokor Hekkus, who almost certainly was responsible for at least one of the kidnapings.

Gersen expressed shock and surprise. Was the old man sure of his facts?

"Yes indeed! There is no doubt whatever! I never forget a face, even though, as in this case, it has been eighteen years."

Gersen's interest began to wane; the old man continued regardless. Certainly, thought Gersen—or almost certainly—this old man could not be a plant by Kokor Hekkus.

"—at Pontefract on Aloysius, where I served as Chief Notator of the Inquisition. He appeared before the Guldounerie, and, as I recall, displayed a remarkably insolent attitude, considering the gravity of the charges."

"And what were these?" Gersen asked.

"Disbursion with intent to suborn ransackment, illicit possession of antiquities, and revilery. His arrogance was justified, for he evaded all punishment save admonition. It was evident that Kokor Hekkus had intimidated the panel."

"And you saw this man yesterday?"

"Beyond question. He passed me on the Route Slideway, proceeding north toward Sailmaker Beach. If by sheer chance I notice this single unregenerate, calculate the number of those I fail to observe!"

"A serious situation," Gersen declared. "This man should be placed under observation. You do not remember his name?"

"No. What if I did? By all odds it is neither the name he used then nor the name he uses now."

"He has a distinctive appearance?"

The old man frowned. "Not notably. His ears are rather

large, as is his nose. His eyes are round and close together. He is not so old as I. However I have heard that the folk of the Fomalhaut planet mature late, owing to the nature of their food, which clabbers the bile."

"Ah. He was a Sandusker."

"He asserted as much, in an extraordinary fashion I can only describe as vainglory."

Gersen laughed politely. "You have a remarkable memory. You think then that this Sandusk criminal lives in Sailmaker Beach?"

"Why not? It is where such unorthodox folk tend to collect."

"True enough." After a few further remarks, Gersen rose to his feet and took his leave.

The Route Slideway ran north, paralleling the Esplanade, then curved through the LoSasso Tunnel to terminate at Marish Square in Sailmaker Beach. Gersen was moderately well acquainted with the area; standing in the square and looking up toward Melnoy Heights, he could almost see the house where Hildemar Dasce at one time had resided. And Gersen's thoughts for a moment became tinged with melancholy. . . . He brought himself back to the matter at hand. Tracing down a nameless Sandusker. It was a problem rather different from that of locating Beauty Dasce, who once seen could never be forgotten.

Surrounding the square were low thick-walled structures of coquina concrete, color-washed white, lavender, pale-blue, pink. In the Rigel-light they glowed as if incandescent, emitting tones and overtones of color, the windows and doorways by contrast showing the most intense and utter of blacks. Along one side of the square ran an arcade housing shops and booths catering principally to tourists. Sailmaker Beach with its enclaves of off-world peoples, each with its typical shops and restaurants, was like nowhere else in the Oikumene, with the possible exception of one or two districts on Earth. At a kiosk, Gersen bought a *Guide to Sailmaker Beach*. It contained no mention of a Sandusker quarter. He returned to the kiosk. The proprietress was a short, fat, in fact almost globular, woman with skin tinted chalk-green: perhaps a Krokinole Imp.

Gersen asked, "Where do the Sanduskers quarter themselves?"

The woman considered. "Not many Sanduskers that I know of. Down the foot of Ard Street you'll find a few. Been requested there because the wind blows the smell of the victu-als out to sea."

"Where is their food-shop?"

"Should you call it food. I call it rubbish. You're not a Sandusker? No. I see not. It's there on Ard Street. Turn down through there—see the two crypt-men in the black cloaks? Right past where they stand: that's Ard Street. Hold your nose."

Gersen returned the *Guide to Sailmaker Beach*, which at once was placed back in stock. Gersen crossed the square, stepped around the two pale men in long black cloaks, and entered Ard Street: an alley rather than a street, running on a slight downhill slant all the way to the water. In the first block were tea houses and curtained game-rooms exuding a rather pleasant odor of incense. Then Ard Street passed through a drab section infested by small sloe-eyed children wearing long gold ear chains, red and green shirts to the navel, and little else. Then approaching the waterfront, Ard Street widened, to become a small court at the sea wall. Ger-sen suddenly understood the pertinence of the advice given him by the fat woman of the kiosk. The air of Ard Court smelled richly indeed, with a heavy sweet-sour organic reek that distended the nostrils. Gersen grimaced and went to the shop from which the odors seemed to emanate. Taking a deep breath and bowing his head, he entered. To right and left were wooden tubs, containing pastes, liquids, and submer-ged solids; overhead hung rows of withered blue-green objects the size of a man's fist. At the rear, behind a counter stacked with limp pink sausages stood a clown-faced youth of twenty, wearing a patterned black and brown smock, a black velvet headkerchief. He leaned upon the counter without spirit or vitality, and without expression watched Gersen sidle past the tubs.

"You're a Sandusker?" asked Gersen.

"What else?" This was spoken in a tone Gersen could not identify, a complex mood of many discords: sad pride, whim-sical malice, insolent humility. The youth asked, "You wish to eat?"

Gersen shook his head. "I am not of your religion."

"Ha ho!" said the youth. "You know Sandusk then?"

"Only at second-hand."

The youth smiled. "You must not believe that old foolish story, that we Sanduskers are religious fanatics who eat vile food rather than flagellate ourselves. It is quite incorrect. Come now. Are you a fair man?"

Gersen considered. "Not unusually so."

The youth went to one of the tubs, dipped up a wad of glistening block-crusted maroon paste. "Taste! Judge for yourself! Use your mouth rather than your nose!"

Gersen gave a fatalistic shrug, tasted. The inside of his mouth seemed first to tingle, then expand. His tongue coiled back in his throat.

"Well?" asked the youth.

"If anything," said Gersen at last, "it tastes worse than it smells."

The youth sighed. "Such is the general consensus."

Gersen rubbed his mouth with the back of his hand. "Do you know all the Sanduskers of the neighborhood?"

"I do."

"I seek a tall man with eyes slightly crossed, who has lost a finger, with hair leaving the rear of his head like a comet's tail."

The youth smiled placidly. "His name?"

"I do not know."

"That would seem to be Powel Darling. He has returned to Sandusk."

"I see. Well, no matter. The money will revert to the provincial treasury."

"Sad. What money is this?"

"A bequest to two Sanduskers who obliged an eccentric old woman. The other is no longer conveniently at hand, or so I am told."

"And who is the other?"

"I am told that he departed Alphanor last month."

"Indeed?" The youth seemed to ruminate. "Who could it be?"

"Again I do not know his name. A man of late middle age with large ears, a large nose, and eyes closely spaced."

"That might be Dolver Cound. But he is still here."

"What! Are you certain?"

"Oh yes. Go to the sea-wall, knock at the second door to the left."

"Thank you."

"It is customary to pay for delicacies consumed on the premises."

Gersen parted with a coin, and left the shop. The air in Ard Court seemed almost fresh.

The sea-wall ran perpendicular to Ard Street; twenty feet below the ocean, translucent and shot like a star sapphire with Rigel-rays, eased up and down. Gersen turned left and halted at the second door: the entrance to a narrow-fronted cottage of the usual lumpy coquina concrete.

Gersen rapped at the door. From within came a halting step. The door slowly opened; Dolver Cound looked forth: a man somewhat older and heavier than Gersen had expected, with a round flushed face and cyanotic lips. "Yes?"

Gersen stepped forward. "I'll come in, if I may." Cound uttered a dismal bleat of protest, but gave way. Gersen looked around the room. They were alone. The furnishings were dingy; a worn purple and red rug covered the floor, and on the cooker steamed Dolver Cound's noon meal. Gersen's nostrils twitched involuntarily.

Cound, recovering his poise, took a deep breath and thrust out his chest. "What is the meaning of this intrusion? What or whom do you seek?"

Gersen gave him a look of hard contempt. "Dolver Cound—for eighteen years you have evaded the punishment due your crimes."

"What's this?"

Gersen brought forth an identification tablet, similar to an IPCC blazer, with his photograph under a translucent seven-pointed star. He touched it to his forehead; the star flashed into light. Dolver Cound watched in loose-mouthed fascination.

"I am a member of the Executive Arm of the New Dispensation at Pontefract, Aloysius, Vega Third. Eighteen years ago you encountered a faulty trial before the Guldounerie. I now declare you under restraint. You must return for a new hearing."

Cound stammered excitedly, and finally in a high-pitched voice cried, "You have no jurisdiction, no authority! Further I am not the man you seek!"

"No? Who must I apprehend? Kokor Hekkus?"

Cound licked his purple lips, glanced toward the door. "Go. Never return. I want nothing to do with you."

"What of Kokor Hekkus?"

"Speak no such names to me!"

"It is either you or he who must settle the score. At the moment he is unavailable. You must come. I give you ten minutes to pack."

"Ridiculous! Nonsense! Sheer balderdash!"

Gersen shifted his projac into plain sight, fixed Cound with a hard stare. Cound, suddenly bluff and hearty, said, "Come now! Let us consider a moment, to learn where you have made your mistake. Sit! This is our custom! Will you drink?"

"Sandusk brew? Thank you: no."

"I can serve less tasty stuff: Sea Province arrack!"

Gersen nodded. "Very well."

Cound went to a shelf, took down a bottle, a tray, a pair of glasses, poured drinks. Gersen stretched, yawned as if inattentive. Cound very slowly brought forward the tray, took one of the glasses. Gersen took the other, scrutinized the clear liquid, seeking the faint roil which would indicate the presence of another liquid, or grains of undissolved powder. Cound watched slyly. He would take suspicion for granted, thought Gersen, and would expect a change of glasses.

"Drink!" said Cound and raised his glass. Gersen watched him with interest. Cound put down the glass untouched.

"Do you not care to drink?" Gersen took his glass, mingled the two drinks, returned the glass to Cound. "Drink first."

"Never before a guest. I would feel shame."

"I cannot drink before my host. But no matter: we will both drink during the trip to Pontefract. Since you do not care to pack, let us be off."

Cound's face crumpled and sagged with woe. "I will go nowhere with you. You cannot force me. I am an old man; not in the best of health. Have you no pity?"

"It's either you or Kokar Hekkus: these are my instructions."

Cound looked toward the door. "Do not speak that name!" he said in an agonized croak.

"Tell me what you know of him."

"Never."

"Then come. Bid Rigel farewell; your sun henceforth will be Vega."

"I did nothing! Do you know no reason?"

"Tell me what you know of Kokor Hekkus. We would prefer him to you."

Cound drew a deep breath, closed his eyes. "So be it," he said at last. "If I tell you all I know, must I still return to Aloysius?"

"I promise nothing."

Cound sighed. "What I know is little enough. . . ." For two hours he asserted the casual quality of his association with Kokor Hekkus: "I was falsely accused; even the Guldounerie panel came to realize this!"

"All surviving members of this panel are under punitive restraint: we are taking a cumulative vengeance. Come now: the truth! I am far from satisfied!"

Cound eventually slumped into a chair and declared himself ready to talk. First however he professed a need for certain notes and memoranda. He went to fetch papers from a drawer, but brought forth a weapon. Gersen, waiting with projac ready, blasted it from his hand. Cound turned slowly, eyes round and wet. He swung his numb arm, staggered to a seat, and now spoke without further evasion. Indeed, he became verbose, almost explosive with information, as if inhibition had been completely dissolved. Yes, eighteen years ago he had assisted Kokor Hekkus in certain operations on Aloysius and elsewhere. Kokor Hekkus had been anxious to obtain certain antiquities. On Aloysius they had raided Creary Castle, Bodelsey Abbey, and the Houl Museum. During the latter operation, Cound had been apprehended by the Sons of Justice; but Kokor Hekkus made certain arrangements, and the Guldounerie panel dismissed Cound with an admonition. Thereupon his association with Kokor Hekkus became less active, dissolving ten years ago.

Gersen pressed for details. Cound waved his arms helplessly. "What is his appearance? He is a man, like us all. There is nothing about him to describe. He is of average size, of good physique, of unknown age. His voice is soft, though when he is angry, it comes as if he were talking through a tube from a far world. He is a strange man: polite when it pleases him, more often indifferent. He is fascinated by beautiful objects, by antiquity, and by intricate machines. You know how he derived his name?"

"This is a story I have never heard."

"It means 'Killing Machine' in the language of a secret world far out Beyond. This world had been settled in ancient days, then lost and forgotten until Kokor Hekkus rediscovered it. To punish the folk of an enemy town, he built a giant metal executioner, which split bodies in half with an ax. As dreadful as the ax was the scream the metal ogre emitted with every stroke. And thereafter Kokor Hekkus was so known. . . . This is all I know."

"A pity you cannot tell me how to locate him," said Gersen. "Either you or he must answer to the authorities at Pontefract."

Cound sat back, limp as a broken bladder. "I have told all," he mumbled. "What can be served by visiting vengeance upon me? Will the antiques be restored?"

"Justice must be satisfied. Unless you can deliver Kokor

Hekkus into my hands, you must pay for your joint misdeeds."

"How can I provide Kokor Hekkus?" asked Cound in the dreariest of voices. "I hesitate even to speak his name."

"Who are his associates?"

"I don't know. It has been years since last I saw him. In those days—" Cound paused.

"Well?"

Cound licked his blue lips. "It could be of no interest to the Pontefract authorities."

"I'll be the judge of that."

Cound heaved a deep sigh. "I cannot tell you."

"Why not?"

Cound made a small, hopeless gesture. "I do not want to be killed in some horrible fashion."

"What do you think awaits you at Pontefract?"

"No! I cannot talk further."

"You have been able to conquer these apprehensions during the last hour."

"Everything I told you is a matter of public knowledge," said Cound ingenuously.

Gersen smiled, and rose to his feet. "Come."

Cound made no move. Finally he said in a low voice, "I knew three men who worked with Kokor Hekkus. There was Ermin Strank, Rob Castilligan, and a man they called Hombaro. Strank was native to the Concourse, which planet I do not know. Castilligan was from Vega's Boniface. I know nothing about Hombaro."

"Have you seen them recently?"

"Certainly not."

"You have photographs?"

Cound would admit to none, and sat watching in limp resentment as Gersen moved here and there around the room, investigating the obvious spots where Cound might keep mementos. After a moment or two Cound said spitefully, "If you knew anything of Sandusk, you would expect no photographs. We face the future, not the past."

Gersen desisted from his search. Cound was squinting at him reflectively; during Gersen's search he had taken time to think. "May I ask, what is your rank?"

"Special agent."

"You are no Aloysian. Where is your throat-hole?"

"No matter."

"If you go around asking questions about Kokor Hekkus, eventually he will find out about it."

"Tell him yourself, if you have a mind to."

Cound uttered a short bark of a laugh. "No, no, my lad. Even if I knew where to complain, I would not. I want no more acquaintance with terror."

Gersen said thoughtfully. "I shall now take all your money, and throw your vile food into the sea."

"What?" Cound's face once more became lachrymose.

Gersen went to the door. "You're a miserable lump of absolutely nothing: not even worth the effort of punishing. I go now. Consider yourself fortunate."

Gersen departed the house, returned up Ard Street to Marish Square, rode the slideway south to Avente. He was by no means happy with the results of his day's work. There was further knowledge in Dolver Cound, had he either craft or cruelty sufficient to extract it. What had he learned?

Kokor Hekkus had been so named by the folk of a secret planet.

Ten years ago, three men named Ermin Strank, Hombaro, and Rob Castilligan had served Kokor Hekkus.

Kokor Hekkus was fascinated by intricate machines; he cherished beauty; he valued the works of antiquity.

Gersen had lodgings on a high floor of the Credenze Hotel. On the day following his interview with Dolver Cound, he arose before Rigel had cleared the Catiline Hills, stained his skin the currently fashionable grayed-buff, dressed in somber dark green, departed the hotel by a side entrance. In the subway system, he voided all possibility of tracker or stick-tight, then took himself to Cort Tower Station. An elevator lifted him to the foyer, where he transferred to a small one-man capsule. As the door slid shut, a voice inquired his name and destination. Gersen supplied the information and added his IPCC Clearance Code. There were no further questions, the car lofted him thirty floors high, moved him laterally, discharged him into the office of Ben Zaum. This was a two-room suite beside the tower's transparent west wall, with an all-inclusive view south over the city and down the coast to Remo. Shelves along another wall held a variety of trophies, curios, weapons, and world-globes. By the evidence of his office, Zaum was a man high in the IPCC organization; how high Gersen did not precisely know: the title "Mandator, Umbria Division" might mean much or little.

Zaum greeted Gersen with cautious cordiality. "You're here looking for work, I take it. How do you spend all your money? Women? Hardly a month ago you were paid fifteen thousand SVU—"

"I need no money. To be candid, I want information."

"Free? Or do you want to commission us?"

"What's information regarding Kokor Hekkus worth?"

Zaum's wide blue eyes narrowed infinitesimally. "To us or from us?"

"In both directions."

Zaum reflected. "He's currently on the red list. . . . Officially we don't even know whether he's alive or dead, unless someone gives us a commission."

Standard whimsy once more, which Gersen acknowledged with a polite smile. "Yesterday I learned the derivation of his name."

Zaum nodded offhandedly. "I've heard the tale. Rather grisly. Might well be fact. Incidentally, to keep you from going stale—" he opened a drawer "—the deweaselers tripped up a man on Palo, and turned him over to Kokor Hekkus. He was returned to us in a condition I won't describe. Kokor Hekkus also sent a message." Zaum read from a slip of paper. "'A weasel performed an unpardonable act at Skouse. The creature you have herewith is fortunate in comparison with the weasel of Skouse. If he is a brooding man, let him come Beyond and announce himself. I swear that the next twenty weasels captured will thereupon go free.'"

Gersen gave a sickly grin. "He is angry."

"Extremely angry, extremely vindictive." Zaum hesitated a moment. "I wonder—well, if he would keep his promise?"

Gersen raised his eyebrows. "You suggest that I turn myself over to Kokor Hekkus?"

"Not precisely, not exactly—well, think of it like this: it would be one man's life for twenty, and weasels are hard to come by—"

"Only the inept are deweaseled," said Gersen. "Your organization is the sounder for their loss." He reflected a moment. "But your suggestion has a certain merit. Why not identify yourself as the man who planned the operation, and ask if he will spare fifty men for the two of us?"

Zaum winced. "You can't be serious. What is your interest in Kokor Hekkus?"

"That of an altruistic citizen."

Zaum arranged and rearreanged several old striped bits of bronze on his desk. "I'm another. What's your information?"

There was nothing to be gained by evasiveness, which Zaum would be certain to sense. "Yesterday I heard three names—men who worked for Kokor Hekkus ten years ago. They may or may not be in your files."

"What are the names?"

"Ermin Strank. Rob Castilligan. Hombaro."

"Race? World? Nationality?"

"I don't know."

Zaum yawned, stretched, looked out across Avente. The day was sunny but full of wind; far out over the Thaumaturge Ocean hung great tumbles of cumulus. After a moment of placid reflection, Zaum swung back around to his desk. "I've nothing much better to do at the moment."

He touched various pads at the console beside his desk. The wall opposite vibrated with a million flickers of white light, then flashed to impart a message:

ERMIN STRANK
Item 1 of 5 entries

with a coded set of physical characteristics below. To the left appeared a photograph with a list of aliases; to the right was a résumé of Ermin Strank's (Item 1) life and works. A native of Quantique, sixth planet of Alphard the Lonely, a specialist in smuggling contraband drugs into the Wakwana Islands, Ermin Strank (Item 1) had never left his native planet. "The wrong Strank," said Gersen.

Ermin Strank (Item 2) appeared. Superimposed in dim pink was the information; *Deceased,* and the date *March* 10,-*1515* .

Ermin Strank (Item 3) had his habitat far across the Oikumene, on Vadilov, single planet of Sabik, or Eta Ophiuchi. He was currently active as a receiver of stolen goods Like Ermin Strank (Item 1) he had never traveled far from his native world, except for two years at Durban on Earth in the apparently legitimate capacity of warehouse-worker.

Ermin Strank (Item 4) was a short spindly knob-headed man of early middle age, red-haired, of truculent mien, incarcerated at Killarney, Vega System's penal satellite, where he had spent the previous six years.

"That's the man," said Gersen.

Zaum nodded briskly. "An associate of Kokor Hekkus, you say?"

"So I understand."

Zaum touched pads on his console. Ermin Strank's (Item

4) résumé was augmented by the notation: *Reportedly asso-ciate of Kokor Hekkus*.

Zaum looked questioningly at Gersen. "Anything more on Strank?"

"I think not."

Next on the screen appeared a succession of Hombaros, the most likely of which had disappeared from view eight years previously and was presumed dead.

The files boasted eight Rob Castilligans. The Rob Castilligan who had robbed Creary Castle, Bodelsey Abbey and Houl Museum, among other premises, was clearly Item 2. There was a recent notation to the résumé that brought Gersen to attention: five days previously, in the Garreu Province of Scythia, halfway around Alphanor, he had been arrested for complicity in a kidnaping.

"A versatile fellow, this Castilligan," remarked Zaum. "You're interested in the kidnaping?"

Gersen acknowledged as much; Zaum brought details to the screen. Seized had been the two children of Duschane Audmar, a Ninety-fourth Degree fellow of the Institute, re-putedly of great wealth. They had been sailing on a lake with their tutor. A surface glider swooped across the water, halting beside the boat. The children were taken, the tutor escaped by diving from the boat and swimming away under water. He had summoned the constabulary, which had acted with great efficiency. Rob Castilligan had been apprehended almost im-mediately, but two other men had won free with the children. The father, Duschane Audmar, had remained aloof, taking no interest in the affair. The children presumably would be taken to Interchange, where they might be recovered upon "rescission" of their "fees" (to use the special jargon of Inter-change).

Zaum's interest was now fully aroused. He sat back, in-spected Gersen with open curiosity. "I take it that you're act-ing for Audmar?"

Gersen shook his head. "A fellow of the Institute? You should know better."

Zaum shrugged. "He's only Ninety-fourth Degree. He might be waiting for a few more degrees before he goes divine."

"If he were Sixty or Seventy, perhaps. Ninety-four is pretty high."

Zaum had thought to detect evasiveness in Gersen. "Then you're not interested in this kidnaping?"

"I'm interested. But this is the first I've heard of it."

Zaum's lips pursed swiftly in and out. "The question comes to mind, of course. . . ."

He was speculating, so Gersen realized, upon the possible involvement of Kokor Hekkus in the matter. He turned to the console pads. "Let's see what Castilligan has to say."

There was a delay of five minutes while Zaum spoke to various members of the Garreu Province Constabulary, another two minutes while Castilligan was brought forward and placed before the Screen. He was a dapper, handsome man, with a smooth easy-natured face, sleek black hair varnished against his scalp. His skin-tone had been washed off; his skin was a marmoreal white. His manner was polite, even cordial, as if he were an honored guest rather than prisoner at the Garreau Carcery. Zaum introduced himself, Gersen remained to the side, beyond the scope of the out-lens. Castilligan seemed amused at the attention he was receiving. "Zaum of the Ipsys. All on account of poor little me." He spoke with the engaging lilt of a Boniface Bogtrotter. "Well then, what can I do for you, beyond baring my life's secrets?"

"That will suffice," said Zaum drily. "How did you happen to be caught?"

"Folly. I should have departed Alphanor with the others. But I chose to remain. The Beyond bores me. I'm a man with a taste for the niceties."

"You'll be quite nicely taken care of."

Castilligan shook his head, with detached and impersonal regret. "Yes, it's a shame. I could apply for modification, except that I enjoy myself the way I am, vices and all. I'd be a tiresome fellow modified."

"Your option, of course," said Zaum. "Still, it's not too bad, if you happen to enjoy the open air."

"No," said Castilligan earnestly. "I've thought it all out, and it's too much like death. Dear engaging Rob Castilligan disappears and with him all *joie de vivre*, all the light of the world; then in stumps tiresome honest Robert Meachum Castilligan, dull as dishwater, who wouldn't steal meat for his starving grandmother. With any luck I'll be back from the satellite in five years or perhaps less."

"Evidently you plan to cooperate with the authorities?"

Castilligan winced impudently. "As little as I decently can, and still get my gold star."

"Who were your confederates in the Audmar kidnaping?"

"Come, sir. You can't expect a man to tattle on his cronies. Have you never heard of honor among thieves?"

"Don't talk about honor," said Zaum. "You're no better than the rest of us."

Castilligan admitted as much. "In fact, I have already bared my soul to the constabulary."

"The names of your confederates?"

"August Wey, Pyger Symzy."

"Kokor Hekkus did not participate directly?"

Castilligan's mouth indented suddenly at the corners. Once more he essayed whimsy. "Now then—why ever should you mention a name like that? We're talking reality."

"I thought I heard you mention gold stars for your record."

"Indeed I did!" declared Castilligan. "But not a gold wreath for my gravestone."

"Suppose," said Zaum casually, "that through your assistance we laid our hands on Kokor Hekkus. Can you imagine the lovely gold star? You'd be elected Honorary Director of the IPCC."

Castilligan blinked sidelong, chewed thoughtfully on his tongue. "You have a commission against Kokor Hekkus?"

"Even if we don't, we could hold him for the highest bidder and earn a fortune. There's fifty-five planets wanting the color of Kokor Hekkus' insides."

Castilligan bared white teeth in a sudden dazzling grin. "Well, truth to tell, I've nothing to hide, because nothing I know could offend Kokor Hekkus. He is as you know, and I can't change the picture."

"Where is he now?"

"Beyond, or so I should think."

"He worked with you on the Audmar kidnaping?"

"He did not, unless he called himself another name. In truth, I've never seen Kokor Hekkus as a man. It's always been 'Rob, do this' and 'Rob, do that' by one or another stealthy means. It's a secretive creature, this Kokor Hekkus."

"In the old days, you plundered museums and the like. Why?"

"Because I was paid to do so. He wanted antiquities, and nothing would do but that daring Rob must rob the sources. Long ago, of course. My salad days, so to speak."

"What of these other kidnapings? How many have you worked on?"

Castilligan made a delicate face. "I don't care to say. It might prejudice my record."

"Very well. How many do you know of?"

"Recently, about fourteen. By recently I mean in the last month."

"Fourteen!"

Castilligan smiled his gay smile. "Yes, it's a going concern. I've asked myself why and wherefore, but—" he shrugged "—who am I to read the mind of Kokor Hekkus? No doubt he, like everyone else, needs money."

Zaum turned Gersen a side-glance, stopped the audio pickup. Gersen said, "What else does he know concerning Kokor Hekkus?"

Zaum relayed the question. The prisoner put on a fretful face. "You play damnably fast and loose with my health. Suppose I told you enough that Kokor Hekkus were inconvenienced—be sure I know nothing of the sort, but assume so—do you think His Horrors would feel kindly toward me? He would learn the dark side to my soul, he would ply me with fears and terrors and all the very ills I dread the most. A man must have some regard for his skin; if he does not, who will?"

"Needless to say, what you tell us will not be communicated Kokor Hekkus," said Zaum smoothly.

"Bah! So you say. A man sits beside you this very instant; I saw you look at him. For all either of us can say, it is Kokor Hekkus himself who shares your office."

"You don't seriously believe this."

Again Castilligan's mood changed. "No. I do not, Kokor Hekkus is Beyond, or so I believe, spending the vast sums he has earned this last month or two."

"Spending how? For what?"

"As to that, I can't say. Kokor Hekkus is old—some say three hundred years, some four hundred—but he maintains a young man's energy. There is no lack of enthusiasm to the man."

After a short pause, Zaum asked: "If you are not acquainted with Kokor Hekkus—how can you know of this?"

"I have heard him speak. I have heard him plan. I have heard him curse. He is changeable, fickle, elusive as a Bernal flame-maiden. He is completely generous, completely cruel—in both cases because he knows no one's mind but his own. He is a terrible enemy, not a bad master. I talk of him like this because it can do him no harm and may help me. But I would never risk offending him. He invents new and special terrors for this very purpose. Yet, should I serve him well, he will build me a castle and make me Robert, Baron Castilligan."

"And where will he perform this romantic fantasy?" sneered Zaum.

"Beyond."

"Beyond," grumbled Zaum. "Always Beyond. Someday we will sweep past the Pale and make an end to Beyond."

"You will never succeed. There will always be a Beyond."

"Never mind. What else do you know of Kokor Hekkus?"

"I know he will be kidnaping other rich men's sons and daughters. He has said as much; he needs a vast sum of money and needs it at once."

CHAPTER 3

From Chapter I, "The Astro-physical Background," in *Peoples of the Concourse*, by Streck and Chernitz:

It is Rigel, that magnificent star among stars, whose prodigious luminosity and spacious Zone of Habitability has afforded the Concourse its existence. Impossible not to marvel at the sheer grandeur of the system! Think of it! Twenty-six salubrious worlds swinging in stately thousand-year orbits around the dazzling white sun, at a mean radius of thirteen billion miles, not to mention the six oft-ignored planets of the incandescent Inner Belt, and Blue Companion, a fortieth of a light-year to the side!

But the very circumstances that make the Concourse what it is provide one of the galaxy's most tantalizing mysteries. Rigel is deemed by most authorities a young star, ranging in age from a few million to a billion years. How then to explain the Concourse, which when Sir Julian Hove arrived, already displayed twenty-six mature biological complexes? By the time-scale of terrestrial evolution, Concourse life is several billion years old—assuming such life to be autochthonous.

But is such an assumption warranted? While the flora and fauna of each planet differ markedly, there are at the same time a number of suggestive similarities—almost as if Concourse life, long, long ago, had a common origin.

There are as many theories to the situation as theorists. The dean of modern cosmologists, A. N. der Poulson, has ingeniously proposed a situation where Rigel, Blue Companion, and planets condensed from a gas already rich in hydrocarbons, thereby giving life a headstart, so to speak. Others, indulging in fanciful flights, have wondered if the planets of the Concourse were not conveyed hither and established in these optimum orbits by a now-dead race of vast scientific achievement. The regularity and spacing of the orbits, the near-uniform size of the Concourse planets, as contrasted with the disparities of the Inner Worlds, give such speculations a measure of plausibility. Why?

When? How? Who? The Hexadelts? Who carved Monument Cliff on Xi Puppis X? Who left the incomprehensible mechanism in Mystery Grotto of Earth's Moon? Fascinating riddles yet to be answered. . . .

Xaviar Skolcamp, Over-Centennial Fellow of the Institute, in a discursive mood, discusses Institute attitudes with a journalist:

"Humanity is old, civilization new: the mesh of cogs is by no means smooth—and this is as it should be. Never should a man enter a building of glass or metal, or a spaceship, or a submarine, without a small shock of astonishment; never should he avoid an act of passion without a small sense of effort. . . . We of the Institute receive an intensive historical inculcation; we know the men of the past, and we have projected dozens of possible future variations, which, without exception, are repulsive. Man, as he exists now, with all his faults and vices, a thousand gloriously irrational compromises between two thousand sterile absolutes—is optimal. Or so it seems to us who are men."

Farmer hauled before constabulary court after attack upon the person of Bose Coggindell, Fellow of the Institute, 54th Degree, in self-justification:

"These chaps have it easy. They lean back in their chairs and say, 'Suffer, you'll love it. Do it the hard way. Sweat.' They'd like me to hitch my wife to a plow, the way it used to be done. So I showed him what I thought of what he calls 'detachment.' "

Justice (after fining farmer 75 SVU):

"A detached attitude toward the problems of others is not illegal."

Of the seven Alphanor continents, Scythia was the largest, the most sparsely populated, and in the opinion of the folk of Umbria, Lusitania and Lycia, the most bucolic. Garreu Province, fronting the Mystic Ocean and backed up into the Morgan Mountains, was the most isolated region of Scythia.

To Taube, a drowsy sun-struck village on the shores of Jermin Bay, came Gersen in the bi-weekly air-ship from the provincial capital Marquari. In the whole town, he found but a single vehicle to be rented: an ancient glide-car with rumbling bearings and a tendency to slew sideways downslope. Gersen inquired directions, climbed aboard the car, and set forth along the inland road. Up a long slope he climbed, with the shimmering Rigel-light drowning the landscape in brilliance.

For a space, the road wound back and forth through vineyards, orchards of gnarled fruit trees, patches of blue-green kale and artichoke, thickets of native berries. Here and there were farm cottages, each with its parasol roof absorbing Rigel energy. The road swung up over a low ridge; Gersen halted to take his bearings. To the south spread the ocean, the foreland sloping up from the bay, the spatter of dun and pink and white that was Taube. In the blaze of light, all the colors of the landscape were unreal pastels, shimmering and dancing. Ahead the road swung over to a level area, where Gersen saw the villa of Duschane Audmar, Ninety-fourth Degree Fellow of the Institute. It was a rambling structure of stone and sun-bleached timber, shaded by a pair of enormous oaks and a native ginkgo.

Gersen walked up the driveway, lifted and let fall a huge bronze knocker in the shape of a lion's paw. After a long wait the door was opened, by a handsome young woman wearing a peasant smock.

"I have come to speak to Duschane Audmar," said Gersen.

The woman surveyed him thoughtfully. "May I inquire your business?"

"I'll have to take that up with Lord Audmar himself."

She shook her head slowly. "I don't think he'll see you. There have been domestic difficulties and Duschane Audmar is not receiving."

"My visit concerns these difficulties."

The woman's expression changed to sudden wild hope. "The children? They have been returned? Oh tell me!"

"I'm sorry—but not to my knowledge." Gersen took a notebook from his pocket, tore off a leaf, wrote: *Kirth Gersen, 11th Degree, to discuss Kokor Hekkus.* "Take that to him."

The woman read the note, without a word departed within.

Presently she was back. "Come." Gersen followed her along a dim hall to a vaulted room with bare white plaster walls. Here sat Audmar with a pad of white paper, a quill pen, a cut-glass bottle of mulberry-colored ink. The paper was blank except for a single line in the looping heavily shaded cursive affected by high fellows of the Institute. Audmar was a rather short man, square-shouldered, firm-fleshed. He had crisp well-shaped features: a small straight nose, narrow black eyes glittering like oil, a compressed mouth over a cleft chin. He greeted Gersen evenly, put aside paper, pen and ink. "Where did you come into Eleven?"

"At Amsterdam, on Earth."

"That would be under Carmand's control."

"No. It was von Bleek, just previous to Carmand."

"Hmm. You were young. Why did you not proceed? After Eleven, there is no great difficulty until the Twenty-seventh."

"I could not submerge my personal goals to those of the Institute."

"And as to these goals?"

Gersen shrugged. "They are uncomplicated, primitive enough to satisfy a Centennial, but centripetal.*

Audmar's eyebrows rose into skeptical arcs, but he dropped the subject. "Why do you wish to discuss Kokor Hekkus?"

"It is a subject in which we both are interested."

Audmar nodded curtly. "An interesting man, agreed."

"Last week he kidnaped your children."

Audmar sat silently for thirty seconds. It was clear that he had not known the identity of the kidnaper. "What is the basis for this statement?"

"I have had an admission from the man who was captured: Rob Castilligan, now in the carcery."

"Your status is official?"

"No. I have no status."

"Continue."

"Presumably you desire the safe return of the children."

Audmar smiled thinly. "Presumption."

Gersen ignored the ambiguity. "Have you received notice of how to effect their safe return?"

"By ransom. The message came two days ago."

"Will you pay it?"

"No." Audmar's voice was soft and easy.

Gersen had expected nothing else. Centennials and near-Centennials were forced to maintain impassivity to any and all external pressures. Should Duschane Audmar ransom his children, he would thereby admit to pliability; he would thus lay himself and the Institute open to exterior persuasion. The policy was well-known; for the tenth time Gersen wondered why Duschane Audmar had been molested. Had he on some earlier occasion revealed flexibility? Had the kidnapers merely blundered?

---

* Centripetal: tending toward centralization or codification; by extension, tending to a kind of fussy officiousness: Institute jargon.

Gersen asked, "You knew that Kokor Hekkus was involved?"

"No."

"Now that you know, will you take steps against him?"

Audmar gave a small petulant shrug, as if Gersen should realize that punitive measures were as flagrant an instability as paying ransom.

"To be completely candid," said Gersen, "I have reason to regard Kokor Hekkus as an enemy. I am not restricted as you are; I can implement my feelings."

In Audmar's eyes appeared a quick gleam of something like envy, but he only gave his head a polite inclination.

"I come to you for information," said Gersen, "and, I hope, whatever cooperation you see fit to provide."

"This will be very little or none," said Audmar.

"Still, you are human and you must love your children. Certainly you do not wish to see them sold into slavery, as they will be."

Audmar smiled, a bitter tremulous smile. "I am human, Kirth Gersen, probably more savage and primitive in my humanity than yourself. But I am a Ninety-fourth, I have too much strength, I must be careful how I apply it. Hence—" he made a gesture indicating a whole complex of ideas.

"Stasis?" suggested Gersen.

Audmar forbore to answer the jibe. He said evenly, "Regarding Kokor Hekkus I know nothing—or at least no more than what is common knowledge."

"Currently," said Gersen, "he seems the most active of the Demon Princes. He creates vast misery."

"He is a vile creature."

"Do you know why Kokor Hekkus took your children?"

"I presume to obtain money."

"How much ransom does he ask?"

"A hundred million SVU."

Gersen, startled, had nothing to say. Audmar smiled grimly. "Not that my little Daro and Wix aren't worth as much and a great deal more."

"You could pay this much?"

"If I chose. Money is no problem." Audmar turned back toward the pad and the quill pen; Gersen sensed that his patience was wearing thin. "In this last month," said Gersen, "Kokor Hekkus has kidnaped at least twenty persons, perhaps more. This was the last reckoning made by the IPCC before I left Avente. The victims are all people of great wealth and power."

"Kokor Hekkus becomes rash," said Audmar indifferently.

"Exactly. What are his purposes? Why, suddenly, does he need such vast sums of money?"

Audmar's interest was aroused. Then, sensing the direction of the argument, he darted Gersen a sudden sharp glance.

Gersen said, "Kokor Hekkus seems to have some large project in mind. I don't think he plans to retire."

"Not after two hundred and eighty-two years."

It occurred to Gersen that Audmar knew rather more concerning Kokor Hekkus than he pretended. "It seems that Kokor Hekkus has expenses of two billion SVU—assuming that all the ransoms run as high as the one assessed against you. Why does he need the money? Is he building a fleet of warships? Is he reconstructing a planet? Is he founding a university?"

Audmar heaved a deep wistful sigh. "You believe he has some large and possibly dystrophic end in view?"

"Why else would he suddenly require so much money?"

Audmar frowned, shook his head fretfully. "It would be a shame to thwart Kokor Hekkus. But from my point of view, and also Institute policy. . . ." His voice dwindled to nothing.

"They are at Interchange?"

"Yes."

"Perhaps you are unfamiliar with Interchange procedure. First travel time is calculated, to which fifteen days is added; during this period only the so-called party of primary interest may rescind the fee. After this time elapses, anyone who wishes may do so. If I had a hundred million SVU, I could do so."

Audmar studied him a moment. "Why should you wish to do so?"

"I want to know why Kokor Hekkus needs so much money. I want to learn many things about Kokor Hekkus."

"Your motives, I take it, are not dispassionate curiosity?"

"My motives are beside the point. What I can do is this. If I were to come into possession of a hundred million SVU, plus my expenses, I would proceed to Interchange and, as a free agent, take custody of your children. Incidentally, how old are they?"

"Daro is nine, Wix is seven."

"Meanwhile I would try to ascertain Kokor Hekkus' motives, his goals, and his current whereabouts."

"And then?"

"After learning as much as possible, I would bring you

your children and if you were interested, report to you what I had learned."

Audmar's face was utterly expressionless. "What is your current address?"

"I am at the Hotel Credenze, in Avente."

Audmar rose to his feet. "Very well. You are an Eleventh. You know what must be done. Find why Kokor Hekkus needs this large sum of money. He is an inventive and imaginative man—a constant source of wonder. The Institute finds him remarkable and regards certain by-products of his evil rewarding. I can say no more."

Gersen left the room without further ado. In the quiet main hall, he found the woman who had admitted him. She turned him a glance of searching inquiry. Gersen asked, "You are the mother of the children?"

She made no direct answer. "Are they—are they well?"

"I would think so. Will you give me photographs?"

She went to a shelf. The boy was smiling, the girl was grave. The woman could not trust herself to speak aloud, and so spoke in a half-whisper. "What will happen to them?"

Gersen suddenly realized that she took him to be a representative of the kidnapers. How did one disclaim such an imputation before it had been spoken? He said awkwardly, "I know very little of the matter; that is, I'm not personally involved. But I hope that somehow. . . ." The only words he could think of were either meaningless or overly explicit.

She went on, "I know how it is, that we must detach ourselves. . . . But it seems hardly fair to the little ones. If there were something I could do. . . ."

"I don't like to raise your hopes," said Gersen, "but perhaps your children will be returned."

She said simply, "I will be grateful."

Gersen went from the cool dim house, out into the sudden blaze of the garden. The afternoon was quiet; when he started the old slide-car, the rumble of the engine seemed intrusively loud. Gersen was glad to put the house of Duschane Audmar behind him. For all its magnificent prospect, for all the charm of its design, it was a house of silence and sternly repressed emotion, where anger and grief must be borne in secret. "Which is why I never went into Twelfth," Gersen told himself.

Three days later, a package was delivered to Gersen at the Credenze Hotel. Opening it he found within eighteen packets of fresh Bank of Rigel notes, totaling one hundred and one

million SVU. Gersen tested them with his fake-meter: all
were genuine.

Gersen immediately checked out of his hotel, rode by subway to the spaceport, where his battered old 9B Locater
awaited him. An hour later, he had departed Rigel and was
in space.

CHAPTER 4

From *The Moral Essence of Civilization*, by Calvin V. Calvert:

> In a sense the explosion of man across the galaxy must be considered a regression of civilization. On Earth, after many thousand years of effort, men had developed a consensus as to what constituted good and evil. When men departed Earth, they left behind this consensus as well. . . .

From *Human Institutions*, by Prade (Textbook, tenth and eleventh grades):

> Interchange is another of the strange accommodations necessary to the functioning of what we have termed 'the total mechanism.' It is a fact that kidnaping for ransom is a common crime, owing to the ease by which escape via spaceship can be effected. In the past, the system for paying ransom often broke down, owing to the hatreds and suspicions inevitably generated, and many boys and girls were never returned to their homes. Hence the necessity for Interchange, which is to be found on Sasani, a planet in the near Beyond, and functions as a broker between kidnaper and those paying ransom. Interchange guarantees good faith in the transaction. The kidnaper receives his money minus the Interchange fee; the victim is restored safely to his home. . . . Interchange is officially denounced but practically tolerated; since it is believed that conditions would be far worse in its absence. Occasionally certain groups discuss the feasibility of commissioning the IPCC to stage a raid upon Interchange; somehow nothing ever comes of it.

Interchange was a cluster of buildings at the base of a rocky hillock in the Da'ar-Rizm, a desert of the planet Sasani, Aquila GB 1201; IV, to use the geocentric nomenclature still favored by the *Star Directory*. At one time in the far past, an intelligent race had peopled at least the two north continents of Sasani, for here were to be found the crumble of monumental castles and keeps.

Private spacecraft were banned from the Da'ar-Rizm, and a ring of cannon emplacement enforced the structure. Persons employing the facilities of Interchange were required to land at Nichae on the shore of the shallow Calopsid Sea, board an airship for Sul Arsam—no more than a station in the desert—then ride a jolting surface car across twenty miles of desert to Interchange.

When Gersen arrived at Sul Arsam, a cold drizzle was dampening the desert soil, and even as he walked from airstrip to depot, vivid patches of lichen appeared. Halfway along the path, a small humming object struck his cheek and immediately set to work tearing at his skin. Gersen cursed, slapped, brushed it away. He noticed his fellow-passengers similarly engaged, and also discerned a sly smile on the face of the depot attendant, who wore what appeared to be an ultra-sonic bug-repeller.

With five other passengers, Gersen waited in the depot: no more than a long shed with screened sides. The drizzle became a brief drenching downpour, then halted, and suddenly sunlight struck down at the desert, raising wisps of vapor. The lichen erupted spores in little pink spurts.

The shuttle-bus appeared, a lumbering crude contraption on four big wheels. It parked an almost purposefully inconvenient two hundred feet from the depot; flapping hands and running to avoid the insects, Gersen and the other five took themselves aboard.

For half an hour, the bus bumped and jerked across the barrens; then in the distance appeared Interchange: low concrete structures around a tumble of crumbling red. sandstone. A grove of feathery yellow, brown, and red trees covered the top of the hill, where three or four cottages were visible.

The bus rumbled into a compound, halted; the passengers alighted and were directed by yellow arrows into a reception room. Behind a counter, making entries in a manual, sat a small sallow clerk with white hair carefully waxed up around a gray skull-cap, the front of which displayed the Interchange emblem: a pair of clasped hands. Waving the group to seats, he continued with his work. Finally, closing the manual with a snap, he looked up, pointed a finger.

"You , sir. I will attend to you, if you will come forward."

The individual selected was a saturnine black-haired man

wearing the tight black jacket and white breeches of Bernal. The clerk brought forward a form: "Your name?"

"Rank Olguin 92, File Mettier 6."

"You wish to redeem whom?"

"Rank Sett 44, File Mettier 7."

"The fee to be rescinded?"

"Twelve thousand five hundred SVU."

"You are agent, principle, or noncommitted?"

"I am agent."

"Very well. Produce the fee, if you please."

The money was brought forward; the clerk counted it with great care, passed it through the slot of a fake-meter, and so convinced himself of its authenticity. He wrote a receipt, requested a counter-receipt, which the Bernalese refused to supply until the redeemed individual was brought before him. The clerk sat back at this display of waywardness, inspected the Bernalese narrowly. "You fail to comprehend, sir. The watchword at Interchange is integrity. The fact that I allow you to produce your money is sufficient guarantee that the guest whose fee you are rescinding is at hand, and in good condition. By your hesitancy and suspicion, you not only asperse our reputation but also tarnish the luster of your own quality."

The Bernalese shrugged, unimpressed by the clerk's peroration. Nevertheless he signed the counter-receipt. The clerk nodded stiffly, touched a button, and an attendant in a red jacket came to conduct the Bernalese to a waiting room.

The clerk shook his head disparagingly, pointed arbitrarily at another of the visitors: this a stocky scowling man with dark-buff skin-tone, wearing the more or less standardized spaceman's garb, such as Gersen's own, which gave no clue as to his place of origin.

The clerk was not impressed by his truculent mien. "Name?"

"None of your affair."

The clerk once again leaned back in his chair. "Eh now? What's this? I require your name, sir."

"Call me Mr. Inconnu."

The clerk glared. "This organization operates without guile or circumvention and appreciates a similar attitude in our business associates. Very well, then, Mr. 'Inconnu.' " With a flourish the clerk wrote. "Who is the guest whose fees you are rescinding?"

"I'm ransoming a prisoner!" roared the stocky man. "Here's your cursed loot; let's have my nephew back!"

The clerk pursed his lips in prim disapproval. "I will expedite this affair, because such is our policy. Your nephew is who?"

"Cader, Lord Satterbus. Bring him forth and be quick about it."

The clerk half-lowered his eyelids, summoned an attendant. "Lord Satterbus, Suite 14, for this gentleman, please." He made an airy flourish, as if dispelling a bad odor, and pointed. "You, sir. I will deal with you next."

The third man was slender and diffident; he wore satin-green skin-tone, the embroidered jacket, the ruffled gaiters currently fashionable at Mountain Wilds on Image, one of the Concourse planets. He wanted to conduct his business in a confidential fashion, for he leaned over the clerk and spoke in a low-pitched mutter—a mannerism the clerk would have none of. Drawing himself back, he exclaimed, "Won't you speak up, sir, I can hardly hear what you say."

The man's diffidence was of no great durability. He lost his temper. "There is no reason why this discreditable dealing must be so public! You should provide booths for those of us with sensibility!"

"Now then, sir," declared the clerk, "you mistake us. You must not expect to slink in here as if you were visiting a brothel. Our service is of the highest respectability. We act as an escrow institution, completely impartial, representing all interests, in trust and probity. So now, sir, speak your business openly."

The man flushed, his skin-toning becoming a muddy gray. "In that case, since you are so open and sincere, tell me this: who owns this business? Who gets the profits?"

"This subject is not at all relevant to our present business," responded the clerk.

"Neither is my name and address. Come now, speak up, since you brim with so much veracity!"

"It is ample to know that this is a corporate body, owned and managed by several groups."

"Bah!"

Eventually the man paid his money and was taken away. Gersen was selected next. He gave his name, declared himself uncommitted: in other words, an independent entrepreneur who might choose to 'rescind the fee'—the usage seemed a special euphemism of Interchange—of a guest who had out-stayed the fifteen-day period of prime redemption, presumably in order to ask a high ransom and thus turn a profit. The clerk nodded curtly. "These are our current 'availables.' "

He gave Gersen a sheet listing several dozen names with the
corresponding rescission fees. Gersen ran his eye down the
list. Near the top he saw:

> Audmar, Daro; 9, male
>> Wix; 7, female
>>> Rescission: SVU 100,000,000.

A few spaces below he found:
> Cromarty, Bella; 15, female
>> Rescission: SVU 100,100,000.

and further:
> Darbassin, Oleg; 4, male
>> Rescission: SVU 100,000,000.

and then:
> Eperje-Tokay, Alusz Iphigenia; 20, female
>> Rescission: SVU 10,000,000,000.

Gersen read the figures, blinked. A typographical er-
ror? Ten billion SVU? An unheard-of ransom, an impossible sum! A hundred million was unprecedented,
though here on this list—he glanced down—were seven
or eight guests with fees established at SVU 100,000,000.
An enormous amount of money but still only a hundredth of ten billion. Something very strange here. Who
could be expected to pay ten billion SVU? It was figure
beyond the budgets of most planets, let alone individuals.
Gersen inspected the list further. After the eight guests
valued at SVU 100,000,000, there was only one other
valued at more than SVU 100,000. This was:
> Patch, Myron; 56, male
>> Rescission: SVU 427,685

The clerk who, while Gersen consulted the list, had busied
himself with another customer, now returned. "Do any of our
'availables' meet your immediate needs?"

"Naturally I want to make a personal inspection," said
Gersen, "but from sheer curiosity, is the figure 'SVU 10,000,-
000,000' correct, or is it a misprint?"

"It is correct, sir. At Interchange we dare make no
mistakes."

"If I may ask, who sponsors this young lady? On whose behalf do you act?"

The clerk bridled. "As you must know, unless specifically
authorized to do so, we must reserve this information."

"I see. Well, what about the Audmar item for a hundred

million, the Cromarty, the Darbassin, the Floy, the Helariope, and the others? Who sponsors them?"

"We have not been authorized to release this information."

Gersen nodded. "Very well. I'll take a look around."

"One more matter, sir. In connection with the Eperje-Tokay item, we cannot allow mere gratification of curiosity. Before you may even inspect this 'available,' you must make a deposit of ten thousand SVU, said sum to apply to the rescission fee."

"I'm not interested to that extent," said Gersen.

"As you wish." The clerk summoned an attendant, who led Gersen from the reception room, along a corridor that presently opened into a courtyard. Here the attendant paused. "Which items in particular would you like to inspect?"

Gersen considered the man. From his flat intonations he was an Earthman, or possibly native to one of the worlds Beyond. He was about Gersen's own age, or perhaps younger, with hulking stooped shoulders, an affable, heavy-featured face toned pale yellow. A cap with the Interchange emblem sat on top a luxuriant crop of wavy yellow hair that swooped behind the ears and back in a drake's tail.

Gersen said in a thoughtful voice, "As you know I'm uncommitted."

"Yes, sir."

"I have a few SVU to invest where it will do the most good. You must know what I mean."

The attendant was not quite sure; still he nodded sagely.

"You can help me considerably," said Gersen. "I'm sure you know more concerning the individual items than you tell the usual customer. If you direct me along the road to profit, then it is only fair that I share with you."

The attendant was clearly intrigued by the direction of Gersen's thinking. "This all seems eminently sensible—provided of course that company rules are observed. These are strict, and the penalties are correspondingly rigorous."

"There is no question of anything not completely aboveboard." Gersen brought forth a pair of hundred-SVU notes. "There will be several more, depending on how much information you can provide."

"I can talk for hours; many strange events have occurred at Interchange. But let us proceed. If I understand you rightly, you wish to inspect each of the guests who are currently 'available?' "

"Correct."

"Very well. In this direction are the Class E cubicles, for

guests whose friends and loved ones are unable to rescind them, and who now—to speak frankly—merely await a slavers offer. Accommodations range upward to the so-called Imperial Gardens on top of the hill. Guests must keep to their quarters during the morning inspection hours, but during the afternoon are allowed recreation of choice, and in the evening there is the social period. Some of our guests find the experience relaxing and own to a sense of gratitude toward their sponsors."

Guided by the now verbose attendant, Gersen examined the miserable specimens in the Class E cubicles, then those in Classes D and C. Before each cubicle hung a placard, with information regarding the inmate's name, status, and rescission fee. The attendant, who was named Armand Koshiel, pointed out various bargains, possible profit-makers and long-shot speculations: "—totally incredible. Look at him, oldest son of Tywald Fitzbittick, the richest quarryman of Boniface. What's forty thousand SVU to him? He'd go a hundred thousand without demur. If I had the sum, I'd buy the fellow myself. It's absolute certainty!"

"Why has not Tywald Fitzbittick rescinded the youth for forty thousand?"

Koshiel shook his head in perplexity. "He's a busy man; perhaps the thrust of business has distracted him. But sooner or later, mark my words, he'll be here, and money will flow like water."

"Very likely."

Koshiel pointed out several other guests in similar circumstances and expressed puzzlement when Gersen remained detached and noncommittal. "I tell you, too much deliberation sometimes leads to disappointment. For instance, there, that very cubicle housed a handsome young woman whose father was dilatory. The sponsor lowered the rescission fee to nine thousand SVU and yesterday a noncommitted buyer—I believe a Sardanipolitan—arranged redemption. And—would you believe it—just as the papers were signed, the father arrived, but was perforce disappointed, since the buyer declared himself satisfied. An unpleasant scene ensued."

Gersen agreed that procrastination sometimes resulted in inconvenience.

"In my opinion," declared Koshiel, "the Oikumene Conference should appropriate a sum ample to meet all rescission expenses. Why not? Most of the guests are residents of the Oikumene. Such an arrangement would facilitate the entire program, and there would be considerably less unpleasantness and deprivation."

Gersen suggested that kidnapers might thereby be encouraged, and Koshiel admitted the possibility. "On the other hand, the situation now existing has aspects that puzzle me."

"Indeed?"

"You are acquainted with the Trans-Galactic Insurance and Guaranty Company? They have offices in many of the large cities."

"I have heard the name."

"They specialize in kidnap insurance; in fact I believe they sell perhaps 60 or 70 percent of all such insurance, for the principal reason that their rates are low. Why are their rates low? Because their clients are seldom kidnaped, while the clients of their competitors inevitably find their way to Interchange. I have frequently speculated that either Trans-Galactic owns Interchange, or Interchange owns Trans-Galactic. An indiscreet thought, perhaps, but there it is."

"Indiscreet, perhaps, but interesting. . . . And why not? The two enterprises certainly seem to dovetail.'

"Exactly my way of thinking. . . . Yes, many odd events occur at Interchange."

They came to a Class B apartment, which housed Daro and Wix Audmar. "Now here's a jolly little couple," said Armand Koshiel. "The rescission, of course, is far too high: these two are worth perhaps twenty or thirty thousand, depending on your taste. Their time of prime rescission is up, they are 'available,' but naturally no one in his right mind would pay so restrictive a fee."

Gersen watched the two children through the one-way window. They sat listlessly; Daro reading, Wix jerking at a loop of string. They were much alike, slender, dark-haired, with the luminous gray eyes of their father.

Gersen turned away. "Odd. Why should anyone post so high a rescission fee? And I notice several other guests with similarly high redemptions. What is the story here?"

Koshiel licked his lips, blinked, looked furtively over his shoulder. "I should not impart this information since it concerns the identity of a sponsor, but I am sure this particular sponsor is quite indifferent. He is the famous Kokor Hekkus."

Gersen feigned surprise. "What? Kokor Hekkus the Killing Machine?"

"The same. He has always given us a certain amount of business, but at the moment it seems that he dominates the entire enterprise. In the last two months, he has brought twenty-six items to Interchange, and all—save one—he values at a hundred million SVU. And in most cases he collects. These children are sponsored by Kokor Hekkus."

"But why?" marveled Gersen. "Does he have some grand project in mind?"

Koshiel grinned a cryptic grin. "Yes indeed. Yes, yes, indeed. 'And thereby hangs a tale,' as the monkey said while describing the cat's rear-quarters." Again Koshiel glanced furtively to all sides. "You may know something of Kokor Hekkus—"

"Who doesn't?"

"—among his characteristics is devotion to the aesthetic ideal. It seems that Kokor Hekkus has fallen madly in love with a girl who—I assure you—is the loveliest vision of the universe. She is nonpareil!"

"How do you know this?"

"Patience. This girl, far from returning the affection of Kokor Hekkus, finds herself appalled and nauseated by the thought of him. Where can she flee? How can she hide herself? The galaxy is too small. Kokor Hekkus is indefatigable; he will seek her no matter where she takes herself. There is no haven for this delightful creature—save one. Interchange. Not even Kokor Hekkus dares to violate the rules of Interchange. First, he would never be allowed the use of its facilities; second, the Interchange management would spare no effort in punishing him. Kokor Hekkus perhaps scorns peril, but he is not rash. So this girl acts as her own sponsor. She establishes her rescission fee at ten billion SVU; indeed, she wished to set it higher, at a thousand billion, but this was not allowed.

"So now! We have this ludicrous circumstance, the girl serene and secure in the Imperial Gardens at Interchange, while Kokor Hekkus sweats and reeks in the extremity of passion. And indeed, he will not be denied. He lacks the cash; somewhere he must find ten billion SVU."

"I begin to understand," said Gersen.

"Kokor Hekkus is by no means baffled," Koshiel declared with verve. "He fights fire with fire. The girl has used the appointments of Interchange to thwart him; he will use the same to gain his will. Ten billion is a large number, but it is only a hundred times a hundred million. So now Kokor Hekkus ranges the Oikumene, kidnaping the loved ones of the hundred wealthiest folk alive! On the day that the hundredth pays the hundred million, Kokor Hekkus will claim the person of Alusz Iphigenia Eperje-Tokay, for she is 'available.' "

"A highly romantic individual, this Kokor Hekkus—in every sense of the word," said Gersen.

Koshiel did not notice the siccant quality to Gersen's remark. "Indeed! Think of it! She must wait, day after day, watching the figure of ten billion become smaller and smaller. Already he has collected for twenty of the guests he has sponsored; every day sees the arrival of more. And meanwhile the girl can do nothing; she is caught in her own trap."

"Hmmf. A sorry situation—at least from the standpoint of the young lady. Her home is where?"

Koshiel shook his head. "As to that, I hear only rumor—indeed the source of all my information. The rumor in this case is beyone the belief of sensible men like ourselves. She is said to have declared herself a native of Never-Never land: the planet Thamber!"

"Thamber?" Gersen was indeed surprised: Thamber, the world of myth, of witches and sea-serpents, gallant knights, and magic forests, was the locale of children's fairy tales. Also, he recalled with a sudden tingle, the home of hormagaunts!

"Thamber indeed!" exclaimed Koshiel with a laugh and an expressive gesture. "It now occurs to me that if you have ten billion SVU and vast courage, here would be an excellent speculation! Kokor Hekkus, if he must kidnap the scions of another hundred wealthy folk, would certainly pay your price!"

"Just my luck to rescind this nonpareil, then have her sicken and die on my hands. Kokor Hekkus and I would both be bereft!"

As they spoke, they had been wandering along the row of Class B and Class A apartments. Koshiel paused, pointed in at a middle-aged man who seemed to be drawing a diagram in a notebook. "Here," said Koshiel, "is Myron Patch, another guest sponsored by Kokor Hekkus. At a rescission of 427,685 SVU, highly over-priced, if you ask me. Unlike the girl from Thamber!" He gave Gersen a lascivious wink and nudge of the elbow.

Gersen frowned in at Myron Patch—an undistinguished fellow of medium stature, plump, with an easy good-natured countenance. The recission fee aroused his interest. Why 427,685 precisely? Behind the figure, behind the enforced visit of Myron Patch to Interchange was a story. He asked Koshiel, "Can I talk to this man?"

"Certainly; he is 'available.' If you think you can mulct Kokor Hekkus of a sum in extent of—what is it? 427,685 SVU, a ridiculous figure—by all means go to it."

"The apartments are naturally equipped with spy-cells and microphones?"

"No," said Koshiel, "and for a very good reason: there is nothing to be gained by listening."

"Nevertheless," said Gersen, "we will take precautions. Let me speak to the man."

Koshiel touched the button that, by ringing a small chime, apprised the guest in question that his attention was required. Myron Patch looked up, came slowly to the front of the apartment. Koshiel inserted a key into a socket; a panel snapped aside; Myron Patch looked forth at Gersen, at first with hope, and then perplexity. Gersen took Koshiel by the shoulders, moved him close to the panel, turned him so that he faced into the apartment. "Now sing: loudly."

Koshiel grinned foolishly. "I know only lullabies from my youth."

"Sing lullabies then, but loudly and with legato."

Koshiel began to yelp a discordant song. Gersen motioned to the even more perplexed Patch. "Stand close."

Patch pressed his face close to the panel. Gersen asked, "Why are you here?"

Patch's mouth drooped. "It's a long story."

"Tell me in as few words as possible."

Patch sighed mournfully. "I am an engineer and manufacturer. I undertook a complicated job for a certain man—a criminal, I now know him to be. We disagreed; he seized my person and brought me here. The ransom represents the money under dispute."

Koshiel started a new song. Gersen asked, "The criminal is Kokor Hekkus?"

Myron Patch nodded dolefully.

"Do you know him personally?"

Patch said something that Gersen could not understand for the fervor of Koshiel's lullaby. Patch repeated: "I said I know his agent, who comes often to Krokinole."

"Can you make contact with the agent?"

"On Krokinole, yes. Not here."

"Very well. I will rescind your fee." Gersen tapped Koshiel's shoulder. "You may stop. We return to the office."

"You are finished? There are others to see: bargains, true bargains!"

Gersen hesitated. "Can I see the woman whom Kokor Hekkus is pursuing?"

Koshiel shook his head. "Not unless you pay ten thousand SVU for the privilege. In essence she refuses to see anyone: even employees like myself, who would be happy to relieve her tedium and relax her understandable tensions."

"Very well then." Gersen produced another three hundred SVU, which Koshiel, bedazzled and dreamy after so much talk of millions and billions, pocketed with a murmur of unenthusiastic thanks. "We return to the office."

CHAPTER 5

From *Popular Handbook to the Planets*,
303rd Edition (1292):

Krokinole: third largest planet of the Rigel Concourse,
          fourteenth in orbital order.
          Planetary Constants:
                Diameter: 9,450 miles
                Mass: 1.23
                Mean day: 22 hours, 16 minutes, 48.9
                      seconds, etc.

General Remarks: Sometimes considered the most
beautiful of all the Concourse planets, Krokinole may
with justice claim to be the most diverse, both geograph-
ically and ethnically. There are two large continents:
Borkland and Sankland; six smaller continents: Cumberland, Layland, Gardena, Mergenthaler, Hopland, and
Skakerland.

Each of these boasts dozens of natural marvels. At
random may be mentioned the Crystal Pinnacles of Bize
Parish, the Card River Falls of Dinker Parish, both in
Cumberland; the Hole through the World of North
State, Sankland; the Undersea Forest off the coast of
Iksemand, Skakerland; Mount Jovah in the Highlands of
Gardena, the tallest mountain (42,102 feet above sea
level) of all the Concourse.

The flora and fauna are complex and highly de-
veloped. The near-extinct Super-beasts, once masters of
the planet, display more than a rudimentary intelligence,
as evidenced by their unique semaphore communicatory
system (to call it a 'language' is to commit semantic
mayhem), their boats, baskets, ornamental knots, and
committee organization.

The human population of Krokinole is as varied as
the topography; again the diversity can only be indicated. Skakerland was first settled by a schismatic cult
of the Skakers who went to Olliphane; in the Highlands
of Gardena dwell the remarkable Imps. Cumberland is
home to the talented and industrious Whitelocks; while

the Druid Banquers wander the tundras of North
Hopland. Other races are the Arcadians, Batthalese,
Singhels, Oporto Fishermen, Jansenists, Ancient Alans,
and many more. . . .

Returning from Sasani aboard Gersen's Model 9B Locater,
Myron Patch explained in greater detail his dealings with
Kokor Hekkus, and indeed elaborated upon the whole course
of his life. Originally a native of Earth, Patch had been a victim of the Texahoma Riots, and considered himself lucky to
escape with his life. He arrived on Krokinole penniless, accepted work as a barnacle-scraper for the Card Estuary
Docking Company, presently established a small machine
shop at Patris, the Whitelock capital. Prospering and expand-
ing, in the course of eighteen years, Patch had become owner
and manager of the Patch Engineering Works, the largest
such enterprise of Cumberland. He had also achieved a reputation for versatility and ingenuity, to such a degree that
when Seuman Otwal brought him a set of bizarre specifications, Patch was intrigued but not surprised.

Seuman Otwal, as Patch described him, was a man somewhat younger than himself, with a strikingly ugly face dis-
tinguished by a long down-curving nose that almost seemed
to meet a sharp uptilted chin.

Seuman Otwal had attempted no subterfuge. He identified
himself as an agent of Kokor Hekkus, and had appeared
content when Patch declared himself willing to work for the
devil himself, provided his money passed silently through the
fake-meter.

With the relationship established on a realistic footing Otwal produced his plans. He wanted Patch to design and
construct a walking fort in the semblance of a monster
centipede, seventy-six feet long and twelve feet high. The
mechanism was to consist of eighteen segments, each
equipped with a pair of legs. The fort, as Seuman Otwal
termed it, must be able to move at a speed of at least forty
miles per hour on synchronized, smoothly operating legs. It
must be able to spurt liquid fire from its tongue, exude noxious gas, and fire energy beams through ports in its head.
Patch declared himself capable of contriving the mechanism,
and, with natural interest, inquired its purpose. Seuman Otwal at first seemed displeased, then explained Kokor Hekkus'
fascination with intricate and macabre machines. Kokor
Hekkus, Otwal went on to say, had recently been victimized

by an obstreperous group of savages, and the fort "would speak to them in a language they understood."

Warming to his subject, Otwal favored Patch with a lengthy disquisition on the subject of terror. According to Otwal, terror was of two varieties: the instinctive and the conditioned. To produce a maximum effect, both types should be excited simultaneously; either alone was capable of being contained. Kokor Hekkus' method was to identify and analyze these factors; then, in his application, he selected and intensified the factors of maximum potency.

"One cannot frighten a fish with talk of drowning!" declared Seuman Otwal.

The exposition continued for half an hour, with Patch becoming increasingly uncomfortable. After Otwal had departed, he wrestled long and hard with his conscience over the morality of building the mechanical horror.

Here Gersen inquired, "Did you ever suspect that Seuman Otwal might be Kokor Hekkus himself?"

"Oh indeed, until one day Kokor Hekkus himself stepped into the shop. He did not resemble Seuman Otwal in the least."

"Describe him, if you will."

Patch frowned. "This is difficult. He has no remarkable characteristics. He is about your stature, he is agile and nervous, his head is neither large nor small, his features are regular and well-spaced. He wears somber skin-tone and garments in the style of the Whitelock elders. His manner is subdued, almost over-courteous, but it is not convincing nor is it intended to convince. All the while, as he speaks softly and listens attentively, his eyes gleam, and one knows he is thinking of the strange sights he has seen and the odd deeds he has done."

There was an interruption now from the two children, who wished to have Rigel pointed out to them. Gersen indicated the white blaze dead ahead, then returned to Patch who continued with the description of his mental turmoil. He had suffered, so he declared, the full range of qualms, misgivings and apprehensions, but at last decided to be guided by two considerations: first, he had already compromised himself, especially since money had been advanced to him, to the sum of SVU 427,685; and second, if he did not build the machine, there were a dozen other shops that would do so. So work progressed, even though Patch was uneasily aware that he assisted in the creation of an evil device.

Gersen listened without comment, and in fact felt no great

disapprobation. Patch seemed an inoffensive individual who had the misfortune to lack an automatic morality.

Construction continued; the fort neared completion. Kokor Hekkus now made his appearance, for the purpose of inspection. Much to Patch's dismay he declared himself profoundly dissatisfied. He derided the leg action, which he characterized as awkward and obviously nonorganic. In his opinion, the fort "would not deceive a child!" Patch, at first appalled, gradually recovered his wits. He brought forward the specifications and demonstrated that he had performed to the letter of his instructions. Nowhere and at no time had he been supplied unambiguous information regarding leg motion. Kokor Hekkus was unmoved. He declared the object totally unacceptable and demanded that Patch make suitable changes. Patch angrily disavowed responsibility: he would gladly make changes but he must ask more money. Kokor Hekkus drew back in outrage. He made a harsh cutting gesture with his hand to signify that Patch had gone too far. Patch, he declared, had not fulfilled his contract, which was thereby void; he demanded return of all moneys advanced: namely SVU 427,685. Patch refused, whereupon Kokor Hekkus bowed and departed.

Patch armed himself but to no avail; four days later he was set upon by three men, beaten in a thorough but disinterested manner, hustled into a spaceboat, conveyed to Interchange where his ransom was set at SVU 427,685. Patch had neither friends, relatives, nor business associates; owing to certain debts incurred in the process of expansion, forced sale of his engineering shop would bring no more than SVU 200,-000. He had given up hope of redemption, and had resigned himself to slavery. Then Gersen had appeared. Patch hesitantly inquired Gersen's motives. He felt boundless gratitude, he recognized Gersen's generosity, but surely there was more to the situation than this.

Gersen felt no impulse to confide in Patch. "Assume," he said, "that I am acquainted with the Patch Engineering and Construction Company, that I consider the ransom as constituting payment for a 51 percent interest in the organization."

Patch rather forlornly declared himself satisfied with the arrangement. "Do you wish formal acknowledgement of partnership?"

"You might write a memorandum to the effect. Essentially I want control over company policy for an indefinite period, not to exceed five years. As to profits I have no immediate need of money and you may apply all such to repayment of the sum advanced."

Patch was not too pleased with the scheme, but had no basis for argument. A sudden thought came to him, and he rubbed his face nervously. "By any chance, do you intend to have further dealings with Kokor Hekkus?"

"Since you ask—yes."

Patch licked his lips. "Allow me at once to register a 49 percent negative vote. If, in your mind, there is even a 2 percent misgiving, the negative votes will defeat this reckless ambition."

Gersen grinned. "All 51 percent cries out in favor of recovering from Kokor Hekkus money illegally extorted from company funds."

Patch bowed his head. "So be it."

Rigel flared across the sky. Gersen located Alphanor; Daro and Wix became effervescent with excitement. Gersen watched them wryly. As soon as they returned to the dim old house in the sun-struck hills above Taube, they would rush to the arms of their father and mother; the kidnaping, the imprisonment, the voyage home would become vague, Gersen would be forgotten. . . . Gersen mused upon the vagaries of fate that had molded him into a—ruefully he supplied the word—a monomaniac. What if, by some fantastic set of circumstances, he succeeded in avenging the Mount Pleasant cataclysm upon all five of the Demon Princes—what then? Would he be able to retire, to buy country land, to woo and wed, to breed children? Or would the role of nemesis have become such an ingrained element in his nature that never could he draw back, never could he know of evil men without wanting to take their lives? It was all too possible. And, sadly, the impetus would come not from indignation or moral outrage, but from reflex, a passionless reaction; and the only satisfaction to be derived would be that of fulfilling a minor physiological need, such as belching or scratching an itch.

As always, such reflections drove Gersen into a fit of melancholy, and during the remainder of the voyage, he was even more terse and gruff than ever. The children inspected him wonderingly though without fear, for they had learned at least to trust him.

Down to Alphanor, down to the continent Scythia, down to the antiquated Garreu Province spaceport at Marquari. Here Gersen communicated by visiphone with Duschane Audmar, whose face was vaguely haggard; Gersen guessed that he had given much introspection to Gersen's mission. He inquired briefly as to the health of his children and accepted Gersen's reassurance with a curt nod.

There was no air-service between Marquari and Taube, and spaceships were proscribed except at the spaceports. Gersen herded the eager children aboard the coast dispatch-ship, a broad-beamed vessel with cargo below and passengers above, which required a day and a night to make the five-hundred-mile run down the coast to Taube. Here he hired the ancient glide-car and rumbled up the long slope to the manse of Duschane Audmar. The children jumped from the car and ran pell-mell, without a backward glance for Gersen, into the arms of their mother, who stood waiting in the open doorway. Her face worked with the effort to hold back tears, and Gersen was conscious of an emptiness within himself, for he had come to feel affection for the children. He entered the house, and now, secure in their home, Daro and Wix ran up, hugged and kissed him.

Audmar came forth, conducted him to the austere room where they had first spoken. Gersen made his accounting.

"Kokor Hekkus needs ten billion SVU. He hopes to raise this amount by extorting a hundred million from a hundred of the wealthiest folk of the Oikumene. He has attained perhaps a third of his goal, and money is rapidly coming in. He desires the money in order to ransom a young woman who to evade him has taken refuge at Interchange under a rescission fee of ten billion SVU."

"Hmmf," said Audmar. "This woman must be extravagantly attractive, for Kokor Hekkus to value her at this figure."

"So it would seem—although any object valued at this figure must be inherently desirable," said Gersen. "I would have inspected the woman, but she, functioning as her own sponsor, charges ten thousand SVU a look, presumably in order to discourage the curiosity of such as myself."

Duschane Audmar nodded. "The information may or may not be worth a hundred million SVU to the Institute, from which the money naturally comes. My children are back with me; I am of course grateful for this, but I fear that I have allowed my emotions to interfere with my reason; I fear that I have compromised myself."

Gersen made no comment. His private opinion was to the same effect. Still, the Institute had only itself to blame; should it choose, it undoubtedly could destroy Kokor Hekkus. "A second matter of interest. The young woman's name is Alusz

Iphigenia Eperje-Tokay. She is native to the planet Thamber, or so she claims."

"Thamber!" Audmar at last was interested. "Is this a serious avowal or facetiousness?"

"I believe that she makes a serious claim to this effect."

"Interesting. Even if all cockalorum." He looked sidewise at Gersen. "You have something else to tell me?"

"You gave me a certain amount of expense money. I used part of it in a manner I considered pertinent: which is to say, I bought a controlling interest in the Patch Engineering and Construction Company of Patris on Krokinole."

Audmar nodded graciously. "It was the obvious thing to do."

"The opportunity occurred at Interchange. Myron Patch was sponsored by Kokor Hekkus, with a recission of 427,685 SVU. The figure interested me; I made inquiry, and when Patch stated that he was able to establish contact with Kokor Hekkus, I redeemed him, taking the partnership as security."

Audmar rose to his feet, walked to the door, returned with a tray containing cordials.

"I find," said Gersen, "that Myron Patch has been building a mechanical monster for Kokor Hekkus: a walking fort in the shape of a centipede of eighteen segments."

Audmar sipped his cordial, held the glass aloft, eyed the rose and violet glintings. "You need not account for the money," he said. "It has paid for a few items of interesting information, and as an incidental concomitant brought two pleasant children back to their home." He finished his cordial, set the glass down with a click. Gersen, understanding more from what was left unsaid than what was said, rose to his feet, took his leave.

Patris, capital of the Cumberland Associated Parishes, rambled and sprawled for miles along the Card River Estuary, with residential suburbs along the shores of Ock Lake. There were many thousand-year-old structures in the Old Quarter: three- and four-story buildings of rough black brick, narrow fronted, with tall narrow windows and high pitched gables. Upriver, in seven-hundred-year-old New Town, stood the famous River Arches: eleven monumental river-straddling structures of a type unknown elsewhere in the human universe. Eight-hundred-feet high they stood: truncated triangles with two-hundred-foot arches carved from the base. Each was identical save for color; each housed shops, studios, service areas in the legs, with apartments for the urban elite above.

Between the arches of New Town and the black brick structures of Old Quarter spread a dingy industrial area and here was Myron Patch's shop. In mingled eagerness, irresolution, pride, anxiety, and wounded dignity, he escorted Gersen to the main entrance. It was a more imposing operation than Gersen had expected, occupying an area two-hundred-feet long by a hundred-feet wide, with parts and material storage above. Patch was depressed to find the shop locked and silent. "It would seem that in a time of stress, one's employees would pitch in, keep the wheels rolling, so to speak, or even make some attempt to rescind the fees of their employer. Over a hundred men and women derived their livelihood from me, and not one so much as made inquiry from the Interchange representative!"

"Presumably they were all occupied in seeking new employment," Gersen suggested.

"Be that as it may, I am not gratified." Patch flung the doors wide, ushered Gersen into the cavernous interior, pointed to the section that had been walled off from the main plant. "Seuman Otwal insisted on absolute secrecy," Patch explained. "I used only trusted employees, and then, at Otwal's insistence, I put them through a hypnotic process in which I ordered them to forget everything they saw in Workshop B after they passed through the door. Also," he said musingly, "while they were in the hypnotic condition I added the suggestion that they work with greater zeal and accuracy, that they feel neither thirst, hunger, loquacity, nor fatigue during the working hours; and I must say that for a space I have never seen such an admirable set of workers. I was about to extend the plan to the entire working force when I was kidnaped; indeed my first thought was that I had encountered bravos from the Fabricators' Protective Guild." He led Gersen across the shop, past various forges, cutters, molds, welding jigs, and lathes, to a door placarded with the universal symbol of KEEP OUT: a red palm-print. Patch ran his fingers over the code buttons to the lock. "Since you are a partner, there can be no secrets from you."

"Precisely," said Gersen.

The door slid aside, the two passed through an anteroom into Workshop B. There was the walking fort. Patch's habit of mild understatement had not prepared Gersen for the ferocious aspect of the device. The head was equipped with six scythe-like mandibles and a collar of long barbed prongs. The eye was a single faceted band; the ingestion orifice was a conical maw at the top of the head with a pair of jointed arms at each side. Behind were the eighteen segments, each suspended from a pair of high-rising jointed legs, these encased in a rugose yellow skin. At the far stern was a nubbin like a second head, equipped with an eye and another set of barbed prongs. The torso had not yet been finished and still exhibited a metallic sheen.

"What do you think of it?" asked Patch anxiously, as if hoping for vindication or endorsement.

"Highly impressive," said Gersen, and Patch seemed satisfied. "I'd like to know what he wants it for."

"Watch." Patch mounted the head of the object, using the prongs as a ladder. He stepped into the maw and disappeared. Gersen was alone in the room with the seventy-six-foot engine of fright. It could spew poison from its prongs, dart fire from its eyes. A sweep of the mandible could slash through a tree-trunk. Gersen looked right and left, then retired into the anteroom. Patch seemed a good fellow, sincerely grateful, but why put temptation in his way?

He positioned himself in the anteroom where he could not be seen from the head, and watched. Patch had started the energy system; the object insensibly had come alive. The head gave a shake, the prongs rattled, the mandibles clicked. From vents at the side of the head came a wild wailing scream; Gersen stood quivering. The scream died. Now the object moved, the legs of alternate segments rising and swinging ahead while the others thrust back.

Backward and forward moved the device, the jointed legs working smoothly if a trifle stiffly. Now the metal centipede halted, pranced sidewise: a step, two steps, three steps. Then the near side of legs seemed to collapse; the object toppled, fell with a clanging thud against the wall. Gersen would have been crushed had he remained in the shop. Unavoidable, doubtless—a flaw in the machinery, a clumsiness on the part of the operator. . . . From the topside maw scrambled Patch, round face pale and clammy, eyes big with consternation. Gersen, watching from the anteroom, would have sworn that his concern was real, that Patch was horrified by the thought of what he might see. Patch jumped to the floor, peered back and forth under the hulk. "Gersen! Gersen!"

"Behind you," said Gersen. Patch jumped around, and if the relief on his face were not genuine, then, Gersen thought, the miming-pads had lost a great performer.

Patch gasped his thankfulness that Gersen was safe. The phasing mechanism for the starboard bank of legs had failed; it was a deficiency that he had not previously recognized. Not that it made any great difference one way or the other, since now the object must be scrapped.

He led the way back into the main shop, locked the door behind them. "Tomorrow," he said, "it's back to work. I don't know what has happened to my old customers, but I always satisfied them in the past and perhaps they will bring their business back to us."

Gersen stood looking across to Workship B. "Exactly what faults did Kokor Hekkus find unacceptable?"

Patch made a wry face. "The leg action. He said it did not produce the effect he desired. The motion was too stiff and rigid. Only a soft supple looping motion would serve. I pointed out the difficulties and the expense of such a system; indeed I doubt if a durable mechanism could be worked out, considering the mass of the fort and the terrain to be traversed, which I understand is extremely rugged."

"My idea is this," said Gersen. "Kokor Hekkus extracted almost half a million SVU from us. I want to get that money back."

Patch smiled a sad tremulous smile. "We should be wiser to ignore him. We do not need his class of trade. Let bygones be bygones, that is the wise course. Come! Into the office. We will go over the accounts."

"No," said Gersen. "I plan to leave these matters entirely in your hands. In the matter of the walking fort, however, I feel that we must regain our money. And we can do it in a safe, legitimate, fashion."

"How?" Patch asked dubiously.

"We must modify the fort so that it functions to suit Kokor Hekkus. Then we will sell it to him for the full original price."

"Possibly. But there are difficulties. He may not now require the fort. Or he may not have the money. Or—even more likely—we won't be able to modify the device to suit him."

Gersen reflected. "Somewhere I've seen a means to overcome the difficulty. . . . Across the Oikumene is Vanello, something of a resort world for the region back of Scorpio. At one of the religious festivals, a platform supported by a long flexible stem raises a priestess dressed in flower petals. Another similar platform raises a table supporting certain symbolic objects—as I recall, a book, a beaker, and a human skull. No matter. The priestess performs rites while the stems twine about each other. I learned that the stems are built up of several dozen smaller tubes, each containing a magnetic slurry: iron powder in a viscous liquid. Reacting to fields from internal windings, these tubes selectively contract with great force. By proper circuitry any contortion of the tubes is possible. It seems to me that this system might be applied to the legs of the walking fort."

Patch scratched his small round chin. "If what you say is correct, I am inclined to agree."

"First we will want to consult Seuman Otwal to assure ourselves that Kokor Hekkus still needs the fort."

Patch heaved a deep sigh, raised his arms, let them flap down to his sides. "So be it—though I would rather deal with adders."

But when Patch called the hotel that Seuman Otwal was wont to patronize, he found that Mr. Otwal was not currently in residence, and the date of his return was indefinite.

Patch heard the news with vast relief. Only at Gersen's prompting did he leave his name and the request that Mr. Otwal call as soon as possible.

The hotel clerk's face vanished; Patch became cheerful once again. "After all we have no need for their filthy money, derived from the most vicious crimes imaginable! Perhaps we can sell the monster as a curio, or even mount seats on the back and advertise it as an eccentric charabanc. Have no fear, Kirth Gersen! Your money is secure!"

"I'm not interested in the money," said Gersen. "I want Kokor Hekkus."

Patch evidently considered this an odd or even perverse inclination. "For what purpose?"

"I want to kill him," said Gersen, then regretted his lapse from taciturnity.

CHAPTER 6

From "Kokor Hekkus the Killing Machine," Chapter IV of *The Demon Princes*, by Caril Carphen (Elusidarian Press, New Wexford, Aloysius, Vega):

If Malagate the Woe can be characterized by the single word 'grim' and Howard Alan Treesong by 'incomprehensible,' then Lens Larque, Viole Falushe, and Kokor Hekkus all lay claim to the word 'fantastic.' Which one exceeds the other two in 'fantasy'? It is an amusing if profitless speculation. Consider Viole Falushe's Palace of Love, Lens Larque's monument, the vast and incredible outrages Kokor Hekkus has visited upon humanity: such extravagances are impossible to comprehend, let alone compare. It is fair to say, however, that Kokor Hekkus has captured the popular imagination with his grotesque and eerie humor. Let us listen to what he has to say in an abstract from the famous telephoned address, *The Theory and Practice of Terror*, to the students of Cervantes University:

". . . to produce the maximum effect, one must identify and intensify those basic dreads already existing within the subject. It is a mistake to regard the fear of death as the most extreme fear. I find a dozen other types to be more poignant, such as:

The fear of inability to protect a cherished dependent.

The fear of disesteem.

The fear of noisome contact.

The fear of being made afraid.

"My goal is to produce a 'nightmare' quality of fright, and to maintain it over an appreciable duration. A nightmare is the result of the under-mind exploring its most sensitive areas, and so serves as an index for the operator. Once an apparently sensitive area is located, the operator to the best of his ingenuity employs means to emphasize, to dramatize this fear, then augment it by orders of magnitude. If the subject fears heights, the operator takes him to the base of a tall cliff, attaches him to a slender, obviously fragile or frayed cord, and slowly raises him up the face of the cliff, not too far and not too close to the face. Scale must be emphasized, together

with the tantalizing but infeasible possibility of clinging
to the vertical surface. The lifting mechanism should be
arranged to falter and jerk. To intensify claustrophobic
dread, the subject is conveyed into a pit or excavation,
inserted head-foremost into a narrow and constricted
tunnel that slants downward, and occasionally changes
direction by sharp and cramping angles. Whereupon the
pit of excavation is filled and subject must proceed
ahead, for the most part in a downward direction."

Seuman Otwal made no appearance during the first month,
nor yet the second. During this time, Patch called his employees back to work, solicited business, and presently the Patch
Engineering and Construction Company was once more in
full clangorous swing.

Gersen took upon himself the modification of the walking
fort. He communicated with the local office of the UTCS,*
mentioned the annual Floration Rite at Vanello, described
the sinuous supports to the forty-five sepalic platforms, and
minutes later received a portfolio of tables, graphs, sche-
matics, and material specifications. He took these to Patch,
who scrutinized them, nodded sagely, said, "Ah, yes. . . . Ah
yes. . . . Ah yes. . . ." After which he heaved a dolorous
sigh. "And so at vast expense, we perfect this ridiculous hur-
lothrumbo to find that neither Seuman Otwal nor Kokor
Hekkus nor anyone else will pay for it—what then?"

"We'll sue," said Gersen.

Patch snorted, returned to a study of the data Gersen had
set before him. Finally he said grudgingly, "The system is
clearly feasible, and will definitely be more flexible than the
jointed legs. However the design of the phasing nodes, the
coupling to the modulators, and the modulators themselves
are far beyond my capabilities. . . . There is a highly
competent group of cybernetic engineers—as I see it, this is
basically a cybernetic problem—a hundred yards up the
street, and I suggest that we contract the whole matter over
to them."

"As you wish."

Two months later, Seuman Otwal had not appeared. After
vehement protest, Patch communicated once more with the
Halkshire Hotel, but Seuman Otwal had not been seen. Gersen began to feel spasms of uneasiness and cast about for another means to make contact with Kokor Hekkus. The fort
itself—so he reasoned—by its very nature should provide in-

* Universal Technical Consultative Service.

formation. He went to the files and brought forth the entire set of plans, specifications, and correspondence, spread all before him.

Nowhere appeared any categorical identification of the planet on which the metal monster was intended to function.

Gersen began all over again, seeking this time for some indirect indication to Planet X, for information implicit in other data.

There was no mention of air-conditioning equipment; evidently the atmosphere was standard or near-standard.

In the specifications, a section read:

> The vehicle must, under full load, be able to traverse slopes of up to 40° (assuming adequate footing) at a speed not less than ten miles per hour; to negotiate easily and certainly broken ground, such as a field of irregularly-shaped rock fragments up to six feet in diameter; to pass across crevasses, gaps, or ditches up to twenty feet wide.

Elsewhere a notation stated:

> Energy requirements have been calculated on the basis of 75 percent thermodynamic efficiency with an over-performance factor of 100 percent.

Gersen set to work with slide-rule, calculite, and integraph. He knew the mass of the fort, he knew the energy required to propel the vehicle up a 40° slope at a speed of ten miles an hour. From this information and the over-performance factor, he could calculate the surface gravity of Planet X—which came to a value of 0.84 standard, implying a diameter of between 7,000 and 8,000 miles.

So far, so good, but hardly definitive information. Again Gersen studied the specifications. They were extremely exact, and allowed no elasticity, with fourteen color sketches depicting the fort from all sides. The object was to be enameled in various shades of black, dark brown, pink, and chalk-blue. Even the enamels and pigments were specified by means of graphs showing wave-length plotted against reflectance. One variable had not been indicated, mused Gersen: the color of the impinging light. Thoughtfully, he called in the plant's color engineer, and requested a set of plaques enameled in accordance with the graph.

While he waited Gersen investigated another idea. The specifications were so exact as to suggest similarity or identity to an actual living creature. The creature would be awesome indeed, but this was consistent with the philosophy of Kokor Hekkus. He prepared a précis detailing the characteristics of the fort, which he submitted to the UTCS. Twelve minutes later, he received a report to the effect that no creature of these taxonomic indexes could be located in the standard references, bestiaries, monographs, or exploration notices. Many worlds hosted creatures with points of similarity: this was a matter of common knowledge. The planet Idora, Sadal Suud XI, exhibited a segmented water-worm, ranging to thirty feet in length; on Earth were various miniature species; the Krokinole Highlands was home to the noxious roof-runner. There was, stated the report, a curious apt reference in an old volume of children's tales, *Legends of Old Thamber*—here Gersen bent suddenly over the sheet. The excerpt read:

> Easing and squeezing, gliding and sliding, walking and stalking: down the mountain it comes on thirty-six supple hooks! Dreadful and dire is the creature in its unhurried haste, as long as the length of twelve dead victims!
>
> "Now we are lost," cried Princess Sozanella. "Shall we succumb to the monster or give ourselves to the horrid Taddo trolls?"
>
> "Hope! Hold to hope!" Dantinet whispered. "For this is the ancient foe of the trolls! It turns its black face away, to look upon the Taddo! It rears to show its blue belly, the color of putridity. The trolls whimper and scream, but too late! And the monster tosses them into its maw. Now we hasten away, through the glooms and passages; for once the Dread has performed a benefit!"

Gersen slowly put down the report. Thamber! Another reference to the world of myth! . . . Xavar Mankinello, the color engineer, came in with tabs enameled to Kokor Hekkus' specifications. Gersen, with as much impatience as he ever allowed himself, arranged them beside the depicted fort. There was an obvious difference. Mankinello bent anxiously over the desk. "There's been no mistake; I took great pains."

Gersen studied the tiles. "Assuming that this is so, what color light will bring the tiles to the same colors as the sketch?"

Mankinello considered. "The tiles are unquestionably cooler than the sketch. Let's step into the lab."

In the laboratory, Mankinello put the tiles under a color

generator. "Presumably you're interested in standard incandescence."

"Standard star-light. I suppose that's close to the same thing."

"Somewhat different, due to the stellar atmospheres. But I can easily code for the stellar progression. Let's start with about 4,000°." He turned a wheel, flicked a switch, checked with a comparator. "Close." He turned the wheel. "There it is. 4,350°." He glanced through a port. "See for yourself."

Gersen peered through the opening. The tiles were now identical to the colors of the sketch. "Color temperature 4,350°: Class K?"

"I'll tell you exactly." Mankinello consulted a reference. "Class G8."

Gersen took sketch, tiles, returned to the room he had preempted for his office. Facts were accumulating. The planet in question attended a G8 star, and was characterized by a gravity of 0.84G. References to the legendary world Thamber had occurred with peculiar frequency. . . . Gersen called UTCS, requested a search for references to the location—hypothetical, fictional, mythical, hysterical, or otherwise—of the lost world Thamber. Half an hour later, a folder was delivered to him with several dozen extracts. There was little of interest, the most circumstantial information being contained in a traditional bit of school-yard doggerel:

> Set a course from the old Dog Star
> A point to the north of Achernar;
> Sleight your ship to the verge extreme
> And dead ahead shines Thamber's gleam.

The information contained in the first two lines might be applied, but thereafter the directions were meaningless. There was no more information to be derived from a study of the fort. Gersen decided that he had come to a dead end. Somewhere in space hung a world where Kokor Hekkus planned to take a metal monster. This world might be home to Alusz Iphigenia Eperje-Tokay who valued herself at ten billion SVU. This world might be the Thamber of myth. But there was no way of knowing.

Myron Patch appeared in the doorway. His round face was taut and accusing. For a moment he looked at Gersen, then said in a portentous voice. "Seuman Otwal is here."

CHAPTER 7

From the Preface to *A Concise History of the Oikumene*, by Albert B. Hall.

Human evolution . . . has never gone in a smooth flow, but always in a cyclical pulse, which, as history is scanned, seems almost convulsive. The tribes mingle and merge to form a race, then comes a time of expulsion, of migration, isolation, differentiation into new tribes.

For more than a thousand years, this latter process has been on the ascendant, as the human race has swept across space. Isolation, special conditions, inbreeding have created dozens of new racial subtypes. But now there is stasis in the Oikumene, with many comings and goings, and it seems that perhaps the pendulum is about to swing back.

But only in the Oikumene! Folk still fare beyond, ever outward. Never has isolation been more easy, never has personal freedom been so cheap!

The eventualities? Anyone's guess is good. The Oikumene may be forced to expand. Other Oikumenes may come into existence. Conceivably men may collide with the realm of another race, for there is abundant evidence that other space-traveling peoples have gone before us, how and why to disappear no one can say.

"Where is Seuman Otwal?" Gersen asked. "Here in the shop?"

"No. Here in Patris. He wonders why I left the message." Patch's expression became more accusing than ever. "I didn't know what to say. . . . Humiliating to deal politely with a man who has wronged you. . . . Swallowing ashes. . . ."

"What did you say?"

Patch made a helpless gesture. "What could I say? Except the truth. That we had worked out a means to alter the fort."

" 'We?' "

"The reference naturally was to the Patch Engineering and Construction Company."

"Did he seem interested?"

Patch gave a grudging nod. "He claims to have new instructions from his superiors. He will be here shortly."

Gersen sat thinking. Seuman Otwal might or might not be one of Kokor Hekkus' various identities; Kokor Hekkus might or might not be aware that the weasel of Skouse was Kirth Gersen. He rose to his feet. "When Seuman Otwal comes, receive him in your office. Introduce me as—as Howard Wall, plant manager, or chief engineer, something of the sort. Don't be surprised by anything I say—or," he added by way of afterthought, "by any change in my appearance."

Patch gave a stiff assent and turned away. Gersen went to the main washroom, where a dispenser offered a selection of skin-tonings. Selecting an exotic duo-tone—purplish-maroon with green luster—he changed his color, and parting his hair in the middle, combed it down over his cheeks in the style of the Whitelock *connoisseur*. He had no change of clothes to complete the transformation, and so donned a white laboratory smock. Still dissatisfied, he clipped on a pair of gold filigree elf-shells over his ears, together with a gold nasal ridge that had been forgotten by one of the more foppish of the engineers. Bedizened and fashionable, Gersen now failed to recognize himself in the mirror.

He crossed the corridor to Patch's suite. The receptionist gave him a wondering look; Gersen walked past her and into Patch's office. Patch, looking up in startlement, hastily concealed the weapon he had been inspecting. He rose to his feet, puffed out his cheeks. "Yes sir? What is your wish?"

"I am Howard Wall," said Gersen.

"'Howard Wall?'" Patch frowned heavily. "Do I know you? The name is somehow familiar."

"It should be," said Gersen. "I just mentioned it ten minutes ago."

"Oh. Gersen. Yes indeed." Patch cleared his throat. "You gave me quite a start." He resumed his seat. "Why the elaborate regalia?"

"For Seuman Otwal. He doesn't know me, and I don't want him to."

Patch's face became dour. "I dislike catering to the trade of suspected criminals; it reflects upon the good name of Patch, and this is our most valuable asset."

Gersen ignored the obvious rejoinder. "Don't forget: I am Howard Wall, your production manager."

"Whatever you like," replied Patch with dignity.

Five minutes later, the receptionist announced Seuman Otwal. Gersen went to the door, slid it open. Seuman Otwal came jauntily forward. His skin was strikingly two-toned russet and black; he had a high-bridged hooked nose, a long sharp jaw and prow-like chin; he wore tall pointed ear-shells of jet and nacre, which gave his head a narrow jutting bony look. Gersen tried to project upon him the image of the man he had confronted on Bissom's End. Was there similarity? Conceivably. Otwal seemed of generally similar physique, but the facial indexes of the two were at variance. Gersen had heard reports of malleable flesh, but here was something more than wadded cheeks or a splayed nose. . . . Seuman Otwal glanced inquisitively at Gersen, then at Patch who had risen uncertainly to his feet. "My general manager," said Patch. "Howard Wall."

Otwal nodded politely. "Your custom must be increasing."

"I was forced to it," grumbled Patch. "Somebody had to look after the business when I was away. I have you to thank for it."

Otwal made an airy gesture. "A matter to be forgotten. My employer has his foibles; he is by no means unfair, though he wants fair value for his generous remuneration. Mr. Wall knows whom I represent?"

"Certainly. He understands the need for discretion."

Gersen nodded with the proper degree of solemnity.

Seuman Otwal gave a slight shrug. "Very well, Mr. Patch. I accept this. So now?"

Patch jerked his thumb toward Gersen, with rather less suavity than Gersen liked, and spoke with heavy irony: "Mr. Wall understands the nature of our previous difficulties and has some new ideas."

Otwal seemed not to notice Patch's lack of enthusiasm. "I shall be glad to listen."

"First a question," said Gersen. "Is the party you represent still interested in the device as specified in the original contract?"

"Such conceivably might be the case," said Otwal, "if our requirements are satisfied. My employer was appalled by the awkward motion of the first version. The legs moved stiffly, with an angular scissor-like effect."

"This was the only difficulty?" inquired Gersen.

"It was certainly the most important one. Presumably the object is built to the well-known quality standards of Patch Engineering."

"Indeed it is!" declared Patch.

"The difficulty then no longer exists," said Gersen. "Mr.

Patch and I have devised a system by which any required motion can be programed and enforced upon the legs."

"If so, and if the system meets our standards of reliability, then this is good news indeed."

"We had best consider the matter of recompense," said Gersen. "Here I speak for Mr. Patch, of course. He wants the full sum of the original contract, plus the cost of modifications and the normal percentage of profit."

Otwal considered a moment. "Minus, of course, those developmental funds already advanced. SVU 427,685, I believe to be the sum."

Patch began to sputter. Otwal could not restrain a faint smile.

"There have been additional expenses," said Gersen. "To a total of SVU 437,685. This must be included in the total reckoning." Otwal started to protest, but Gersen held up his hand. "We do not care to argue this point. We are prepared to deliver the mechanism, but we insist upon payment, which is as I stated it. Of course, if your principal wishes to make further representations, we shall be glad to listen to him in person."

Otwal gave a cool laugh. "No matter: I agree. My principal is anxious to take delivery."

"Still—and no denigration intended—we would prefer to deal with your principal, in order to minimize all misunderstanding."

"Impossible. He is involved elsewhere. But why be concerned over trifles? I have full power to act on his behalf."

Patch began to make restless movements; his prerogatives were ruthlessly being accroached by this so-called partner, whose only contribution to Patch Engineering and Construction was the rescission at Interchange. Gersen kept one eye on Patch and one on Otwal; neither was predictable.

"We accept this," Gersen told Otwal. "Now we need another installment of developmental money—approximately half a million SVU."

"Impossible!" snapped Otwal. "My principal is engaged in an enterprise where he must concentrate all his resources."

Patch began to fume. "You pay me, then you—"

Gersen said hastily, "Assume that the device is completed and ready for delivery: how can we feel confident of collecting our money?"

"You have my personal reassurance," said Otwal.

"Bah!" barked Patch. "That is not enough! You cheated me before, you'd do it again if you had the chance."

Otwal looked pained and turned to Gersen. "If we fail to meet our obligations—a ridiculous speculation—you need only withhold delivery. How simple it all is."

"What would we do then with a thirty-six legged fort?" asked Gersen. "No. We must insist on one-third payment now, another third upon approval of the leg action, and the final third upon delivery."

"I think they ought to pay punitive damages," muttered Patch. "Ten thousand isn't enough. It should be a hundred thousand. Two hundred thousand. My discomfort, my anxiety, my—"

Wrangling continued. Otwal demanded details as to the new leg action; Gersen replied in diffuse terms: "We use flexible members shaped precisely to specifications. They are actuated by hydraulic tubes of a special variety, controlled by electrical modulations of infinite range."

Otwal finally gave in. "We could easily take our business to another concern—but time is of the essence. When will you guarantee delivery? There must be a penalty clause in the new contract: we have already been far too lenient."

Again disputation ensued, and at one point Patch rose to his feet, leaned forward over his desk to shake his fist; Otwal disdainfully drew back apace.

The matter finally was adjusted. Otwal insisted upon seeing the half-completed fort, and, grumbling, Patch led the way with Gersen bringing up the rear. As he walked, Gersen studied Otwal's form: a man with the light sure tread of a panther, broad in the shoulder, narrow of hip—very like Billy Windle, but also like millions of other active and muscular men.

Otwal was surprised to find technicians already hard at work. He turned to Gersen with a rueful grin. "You anticipated my agreement?"

"Certainly—after driving the hardest bargain possible."

Otwal laughed. "An accurate appraisal of the situation. You are a clever man, Mr. Wall. Have you ever been Beyond?"

"Never. I am orthodox and unadventurous."

"Strange," said Seuman Otwal. "There is a certain air, almost an emanation, that clings to those who have worked Beyond. I thought I sensed it in you. Of course I am often wrong in my suppositions." He turned back to the fort.

"Well, everything seems to be correct, except of course for the surface finish."

"To satisfy our curiosity," said Gersen, "perhaps you can describe its ultimate purpose."

"Certainly. My principal spends a good deal of time on a remote planet beset with barbarians. When he wishes to go abroad, they harass him severely. He wants security and this the fort will provide."

"Then the fort is purely defensive in nature?"

"Of course. My principal is a much-maligned man. I find him quite reasonable. He is daring, enterprising, even reckless, and certainly the most imaginative man alive—but in all aspects reasonable."

Gersen nodded thoughtfully. "I understand that he makes an imaginative use of the force of terror."

"Far better the fear of an act," Otwal stated, "than the brutal act itself. Do you not agree?"

"Possibly. But it occurs to me that a man so obsessed with the abstract notion of terror must suffer inordinate terrors on his own account."

Otwal seemed startled. "I had not considered this," he said. "I think that I agree. An emphatic man lives a hundred lives; he senses joys, sorrows, triumphs, despairs and, yes, terrors, beyond the horizon of the common man. He exults greatly, he suffers greatly, he fears greatly, but never would he arrange matters differently."

"What would you consider his supreme fear?"

"It is no secret: death. He fears nothing else—and in fact has taken extravagant steps to avoid it."

"You speak with great authority," mused Gersen. "You know Kokor Hekkus well?"

"As well as anyone. And of course I am an imaginative man in my own right."

"I also," declared Patch, "still I do not conduct my financial business through Interchange."

Seuman Otwal laughed quietly. "A sad episode that I suggest we consign to the past, and forget forever."

"Easy for you to say," Patch complained. "You weren't locked up away from your business for over two months."

They returned to the office where Otwal, rather gloomily, so it seemed, signed a bank voucher on a numbered account for the sum of half a million SVU; then, once more gracious, departed. Gersen immediately took the money to the local branch of the Bank of Rigel, where the check was verified and the money credited to the account of Patch Construction.

When he returned to the shop, he found Patch in a belligerent mood. Patch wanted Gersen to take the advance from Otwal and relinquish his partnership, but Gersen refused to agree. Patch muttered darkly about agreements negotiated under duress, and spoke of closing the shop until the law set matters straight. Gersen laughed at him. "You can't close the shop. I own a controlling interest."

"I didn't realize I was dealing with thugs and bandits," blurted Patch. "I didn't realize that the good name of Patch Construction would be tainted. Monsters! Murderers! Terrorists! Thieves! Robbers! What have I let myself in for?"

"Eventually you'll have your shop back," Gersen consoled him. "And don't forget—there'll be a handsome profit for Patch Construction."

"Unless I get snatched off to Interchange again," said Patch bleakly. "I expect nothing better."

Gersen uttered a soft quiet curse, and Patch looked in wonder to see Gersen evince an overt sign of emotion. "What's the trouble?"

"Something I neglected, something I never considered."

"And what is that?"

"I might have put a stick-tight on Seuman Otwal—or followed him."

"Why bother? He stays at the Halkshire Hotel. Seek him there."

"Yes, of course," Gersen went to the visiphone, was connected with the Halkshire front desk. He was informed that Mr. Otwal was not in residence at the moment, but that a message would eventually reach him. Gersen turned back to Patch. "Suspicious rascal. He probably would have ducked my stick-tight."

Patch was now studying Gersen with a new and intent expression. "I knew it all along."

"What?"

"You're an Ipsy agent."

Gersen laughed, shook his head. "I'm just ordinary Kirth Gersen."

"How," asked Patch with a shrewd grin, "can you get the use of a stick-tight operation if you're not police or Ipsy?"

"No great problem, if you know the right people. Let's get on with our monster."

On the following day, Seuman Otwal called by visiphone to state that he was leaving the planet. He would return in perhaps two months, when he hoped to see substantial progress.

On the day following, there was sensational news. In the course of one night, five of the wealthiest families of Cumberland had suffered the kidnaping of one or more of their members. "Such was Seuman Otwal's business on Krokinole," Gersen told Patch.

The fort progressed with satisfactory rapidity—a fact that pleased Patch but troubled Gersen. Either Seuman Otwal was Kokor Hekkus or he was not. If not, how could he be forced to reveal Kokor Hekkus' whereabouts? Gersen's best hope was that Kokor Hekkus, in his own guise, might once more visit the shop. If not . . . Gersen toyed with the idea of a secret capsule aboard the fort in which to stow away, but rejected the idea: the fort was far too small. . . . Might he arrange to accompany the fort as instructor or expert? If the fort were truly bound for Thamber, he might find himself effectually exiled for life, or enslaved.

An idea on a different level occurred to him, which during the next few days he took steps to implement. The control pulses from the fort's cycling mechanism ran through a dorsal duct, branching off right and left to the relays in each segment. Where the duct passed back across the head, Gersen introduced a cut-off switch, activated by cells on either side of the head. If the gas within these cells were ionized—say by the impact of a weak projac beam—electricity flowing across the cell would open the switch, rendering the fort immobile for at least ten minutes.

Meanwhile the surface enamels had been applied. The engines and circuits were checked and adjusted, the leg action tested under various types of cycles; and then the fort was adjudged complete. In the dim hours of early morning, it was shrouded under canvas, walked out into the street, to be grappled by a freight copter and conveyed to a wild area at the south of the Bize Parish Barrens for field trials. Patch proudly sat at the controls, Gersen rode beside him. The fort rambled smoothly over rough ground and shrubs, climbed hills without faltering. Certain maladjustments made themselves known, and were taken note of. A few minutes before noon, the fort breasted a low ridge and scuttled down into the camp of a Natural Life Association party. A hundred nature lovers looked up from their noon meal, emitted simultaneous gasps of horror and fled screaming over the hills.

"Another success," said Gersen. "We can now with candor guarantee frightfulness to Kokor Hekkus."

Patch halted the fort, turned it about, drove it back over the ridge. At twilight it was once again draped in canvas, and carried back to the shop.

Almost as if Seuman Otwal were clairvoyant, he called on the following day to request a progress report. Patch assured him that all went well; that if he so chose he could undertake a test of the fort on the following day. Otwal agreed and once again the fort was shrouded, trundled out into the predawn stillness, and conveyed into the badlands behind the Crystal Pinnacles, with Otwal following in a small nondescript air-car.

Gersen, wearing his maroon duo-tone and fashionable accouterments, took the controls, and once again the fort ran smartly up and down the foothills.

Weaponry, by the terms of the contract, had not been installed; however the gas sacs and odoriferous glands had been loaded with smoke-gas and colored water; they spouted and sprayed with precision and accuracy. Otwal alighted, stood while the fort trundled back and forth, then returned to the head compartment and took over the controls. He said very little but his attitude indicated approval. Patch, likewise silent, was clearly congratulating himself that the entire odious adventure would soon be at an end.

At dusk, the fort once more was conveyed back to Patris. Otwal, Patch, and Gersen gathered in Patch's office. Otwal walked back and forth as if in deep thought. "The fort seems to perform well enough," he said, "but to be perfectly frank, I consider the price somewhat high. I shall recommend to my principal that he inspect the mechanism only if the price is reduced to a reasonable and rational figure."

Patch reeled back and went red in the face. "What!" he roared. "Do you dare stand here and say that? After all our suffering, all we've been through to produce the damnable thing?"

Seuman Otwal inspected Patch coldly. "It serves nothing to rant. I have explained my—"

"The answer is no! Out of here! Don't come back till you bring every cursed coin we have owing!" Patch marched forward. "Get out, or I'll throw you out! Nothing could give me more pleasure. In fact—" he seized Otwal by the shoulder and hustled him about. Otwal swayed, smiled serenely toward Gersen, as if in amusement for the playful ferocity of a kitten. Patch tugged again; Otwal moved slightly; Patch was flung across the room, to strike his head against his desk and lie blinking. Otwal turned to Gersen. "What of you? Do you care to try your luck?"

Gersen shook his head. "I only want to wind up the contract. Bring your principal for his final inspection, then if he is satisfied, take delivery. Under no circumstances will we reduce our price; in fact, we now must start to charge interest upon the amount owing."

Seuman Otwal laughed, glanced at Patch who was slowly raising himself to a sitting position. "You take a strong position. Under the circumstances I might do the same. Very well; I am forced to agree. When can the fort be delivered?"

"According to the terms of our contract, we must pack it in foam, crate it, and convey it to the spaceport—a matter of three days after final acceptance and payment."

Seuman Otwal bowed. "Very well. I will try to make contact with my principal, after which I will render the requisite notification."

"I believe," said Gersen, "that a second payment is now due." Patch was rubbing his head, staring in virulent hate toward Seuman Otwal. "Why bother?" said Seuman Otwal carelessly. "Let us handle these tiresome financial matters later."

Gersen refused to agree. "What good is a contract if the terms are not intended to be binding?" Patch struggled to his feet, moved with an air of purpose around behind his desk. Gersen stepped quickly past, removed the projac from the half-open drawer. Otwal laughed negligently. "You just saved his life."

"I saved our second payment," said Gersen, "because I would have been forced to kill you as well."

"No matter, no matter. Let us not talk of death, horrid to consider nonbeing! You want your money; tiresome people. Another half million, I presume?"

"Correct. And a final payment of—" Gersen consulted notes "—of SVU 681,490, which will settle accounts in full with Patch Construction."

Otwal walked slowly back and forth. "I will have to make arrangements. . . . Three days to crate and foam, you say?"

"That seems a reasonable period."

"It is too long. Here is how we shall simplify. Cover the fort with the tarpaulin; at midnight walk it out into the street.

A freight-carrier will grapple to it, and take it to our cargo ship, which is by chance convenient."

"There is one difficulty," said Gersen. "The banks will be closed, and your check cannot be certified."

"I will bring the money in cash, all of it: second and third payments together."

Essentially Gersen cared not a whit for the money; but suddenly it seemed important not to let Seuman Otwal hood-wink Patch Construction a second time. He forced himself to consider the situation from a larger perspective. He asked cautiously, "What of your principal?"

Seuman Otwal made an impatient gesture. "I will take my chances with him. He is occupied elsewhere and has given me full competence. Come; what do you say?"

Gersen smiled sourly. Was this hawk-faced man Kokor Hekkus—or not? Sometimes it seemed indubitably yes, and the next moment as certainly no. Gersen temporized. "One more matter—that of service. Do you expect us to provide a technical expert?"

"If it becomes necessary, you will be notified. But after all, our own technical staff is at hand, and indeed is responsible for the design. I foresee no need for any such expert."

Patch lurched upright in his chair. "Get out," he muttered thickly. "Get out, both of you. Murderers, thugs. You too, Wall, or Gersen, or whatever your name is. I don't know what your game is, but get out."

Gersen turned him a casual glance, then ignored him. Seuman Otwal seemed amused. Gersen said, "If you want to take delivery at midnight, pay into our bank account the full sum due us. We want no cash, to be fake-metered and carried around until the banks open. You and your principal of course are men of probity, but knaves and scoundrels are known to exist. As soon as the deposit is verified, you can take delivery of the fort."

Seuman Otwal considered gravely. Then he acquiesced. "It shall be as you wish." He turned a serpent's flick of a glance at his watch. "There is time. Which is your bank?"

"Bank of Rigel, Patris Old-Town Main."

"In half an hour, more or less, you may make inquiry. At midnight I will arrange to take delivery." Gersen, remembering, perhaps belatedly, his ostensible role, turned to Patch. "Does the arrangement meet your approval, Mr. Patch?"

Patch growled something indistinguishable that Gersen and Seuman Otwal graciously assumed to be assent; Seuman Otwal bowed and departed. Gersen turned to consider Patch; Patch glared back. Gersen controlled an impulse to rake him over the coals, and seated himself. "We must make plans."

"What is the needs for plans now? As soon as the money reaches the bank, I intend to buy you out of Patch Construction if it takes every last cent, and then be damned to you."

"You show very little gratitude," said Gersen. "But for me you'd still be sitting in a cell at Interchange."

Patch nodded bitterly. "You rescinded my fee—for purposes of your own. I have no idea what these purposes are, but they have nothing to do with me. As soon as the money reaches the bank, I'll buy you out; I'll pay any additional sum you require—within reason—and I'll say good-bye to you with the utmost joy."

"As you wish," said Gersen. "I do not care to stay where I am not wanted. As to the additional sum—make the total an even half million."

Patch puffed out his cheeks. "That will be eminently satisfactory."

Half an hour later, Patch called the area Branch of the Bank of Rigel, inserted his account tab into the credit card slot. Yes, he was told, the sum of SVU 1,181,490 had been deposited to his account.

"In that case," said Patch, "please open an account in the name of Kirth Gersen—" he spelled the name"—and deposit to this account the sum of SVU 500,000."

The transaction was performed, both Patch and Gersen affixing signatures and thumbprints to tabs. Patch then turned to Gersen. "You will now write me a receipt and destroy the partnership agreement."

Gersen did as requested. "Now," said Patch, "you will be good enough to leave the premises and never return."

"Whatever you say," replied Gersen courteously. "The association has been stimulating. I wish you and Patch Construction prosperity, and I offer you a final word of advice: after the fort has been delivered, try not to be kidnaped again."

"Have no fears on that score." Patch grinned wolfishly. "I'm not an inventor and an engineer for nothing. I have devised a protective harness that will blow the hands and face off anyone who touches me; let the kidnapers beware!"

CHAPTER 8

Favorite dictum of Raffles, the amateur cracksman:

> Money lost, little lost,
> Honor lost, much lost.
> Pluck lost, all lost.

The night of a Concourse planet was seldom completely dark. For those worlds appropriately placed in orbit, Blue Companion served as a small intense moon; the night sky of all the worlds sparkled with at least several sister planets.

Krokinole saw Blue Companion only as an evening star—a state of affairs that would persist for yet another hundred years or so, due to the vast circumference of the orbits of all the Concourse planets and the consequent sluggish annual motion; in the case of Krokinole 1642 years.

Krokinole midnight was as dark as any of the Concourse. Patris, still influenced by the old time Whitelock Injunctionary Procedures, had little to offer in the way of night life; what small nocturnal revelry there was centered in New Town at the riverside restaurants. Old City was dark and damp from the estuary mist, with Patch Construction a bright island.

Half an hour before midnight, Gersen came quietly along the empty streets. Blue Companion had long departed the sky; street illumination consisted of a dim globe at far intervals, surrounded by a golden halo of mist. The air smelled of damp brick, the estuary docks, the mud flats across the estuary: a subtle moldering reek unique to Patris Old Town. Opposite Patch Construction stood a row of the tall high-gabled buildings, each with a deeply recessed areaway filled with shadow. From one to another of these dark alcoves Gersen slipped, approaching the oblong of light projected from the open doors of Workshop B. He came as close as he thought practical, leaned back against the moldering brick, eased the various clips and straps supporting his weapons and set himself to wait. He wore black, with black skin-tone, black eye-shells to conceal the gleam of his eyes; standing quiet he was part of the misty night; a sinister shape.

Time passed. Inside the shop, the forward end of the canvas-swathed fort could be seen, and, from time to time, a technician. On one occasion, Patch's burly form appeared in the opening as he stepped out to peer up into the sky.

Gersen checked the time: five minutes to midnight. He fitted a pair of night-glasses to his forehead, slipped them down over his eyes, and instantly the street seemed bright, though with unreal shadows and tones, the chiaroscuro sometimes reversed, sometimes not. The glare from the shop was compensated by a mutachrome filter, appearing as a dark blotch. Gersen scanned the sky, but saw nothing.

At a minute before midnight, Patch again stepped out into the street. Two heavy projacs ostentatiously hung in holsters at his waist and at his throat was clasped a microphone undoubtedly tuned to the police emergency band. Gersen grinned: Patch was taking no chances. After a suspicious look around the sky, Patch returned within. A minute passed; a long dismal hoot from the Mermiana monument, the female colossus standing knee deep in the sea, signified midnight. High in the sky appeared the shape of a freight-carrier. It settled, then halted in mid-air. Gersen squinted up through the night-glasses, tentatively brought around his grenade rifle. The carrier was presumably manned by men in the service of Kokor Hekkus; the galaxy would profit by their deaths. . . . But where was Kokor Hekkus? And Gersen cursed the uncertainty that restrained him from pulling the trigger.

A small air-car appeared. It swooped and, ignoring the traffic laws of Patris, settled into the street, landing less than a hundred feet from Gersen's hiding place. He pressed far back into the shadows, flipped up the night-glasses, which now would only hinder and confuse him.

Two men alighted from the air-car. Gersen grunted in disappointment. Neither was Seuman Otwal; neither could possibly be Kokor Hekkus. Both were short, compact, dark-skinned; both wore tight dark garments and tight black hoods. They walked with quick steps to the shop, peered into the interior and one made an imperious gesture. Gersen lowered his night-glasses, glanced up to the freight-carrier. It remained as before. Gersen raised the nightglasses, returned to the two men from the air-car. Patch came forward, marching with a swagger of unconvincing truculence. He halted and spoke; the two nodded curtly, and one said a few words into a microphone.

Patch turned, gestured; the fort walked out into the street, the canvas bulging and jerking to the motion of the legs. Down from the sky came the freight-carrier. Gersen watched with the certainty that here the chain of events that had started on the Avente Esplanade was to dwindle and die.

Patch stepped back into the shop, one hand on each of his guns. The two men in black ignored him; down now from the air-ship came a strong-back from which depended ten cables. The two men clambered up to the top of the fort, shackled the cables to eyebolts along the dorsal ridge. They jumped to the ground, gave a wave; the fort was lofted away through the night. The two men went quickly to their car without a backward glance for Patch, who stood bristling and glaring defiance at their backs. The air-car swept off into the dark; Patch and his shop were left, curiously forlorn and bereft.

The doors to Workshop B closed; the street was dark and vacant. Gersen shifted from his cramped position. He felt defeated and angry. Why, at least, had he not shot down the air-ship and the fort? Kokor Hekkus might well have been aboard. Even if such were not the case, the destruction of the fort would have infuriated him, goaded him to some kind of action.

Gersen knew very well why he had not destroyed the fort. Indecision had cramped his finger. He ached for the final confrontation. Kokor Hekkus must know why he died and who killed him. To shoot him down in the dark was good, but not good enough.

How and where to win another opportunity? Perhaps through Seuman Otwal and the Halkshire Hotel. Gersen stepped out into the street. Three dark shapes sprang back in startlement; one gave a hoarse order, and a beam of intense white light flooded forth to blind Gersen. He snatched for his weapons; one of the shapes scrambled forward, knocked down his arm; another swung a long length of black cable; it coiled around Gersen's body almost as if alive, to constrict his right arm and his thighs. There came another coiling length of cable, snapping around his legs; Gersen tottered, fell. His heavy weapons were kicked to the side, his knife and projac snatched away.

The man holding the light advanced, turned it down at

Gersen. He chuckled. "Good enough. This one's the partner with the money."

It was the cool easy voice of Seuman Otwal. Gersen said, "You're wrong. Patch bought me out."

"Excellent. . . . Then you have money."

The light moved closer. "Search him, with care. This man might well be dangerous."

Cautious fingers probed Gersen's person, found and removed a throwing dagger, a prickle-sac half-full of anodyne, several other devices that obviously puzzled the searchers. One said in a voice of respectful wonder: "This one's a walking arsenal. I'd not like to face him alone."

"Yes," said Seuman Otwal thoughtfully. "A strange sort to be frowsting it as an artisan. A strange sort, indeed. . . . Well, no matter. The universe is full of strange sorts, as well we know. He is now our guest, and we need not delay for Patch."

Down eased an air-boat. Gersen was hoisted into the hold; the craft slid off and away through the Krokinole night.

Seuman Otwal presently looked into the hold. "You're a strange man, Mr. Wall, or whatever your name is. You decked yourself out with a variety of weapons, almost as if you knew how to use them; you concealed yourself with such stealthy patience that we, who are also stealthy and patient, had no inkling of your nearness; and then without a look over your shoulder, you swagger out into the middle of the street."

"It was a poor move," Gersen agreed.

"The initial folly was your partnership with Patch—and this is useless to deny as we have informed ourselves—when it should have been apparent that never would the bumptious Patch be paid for the fort. He was forced to disgorge at Interchange; now it is your turn. If you can tender us our SVU 1,681,490 at once, we will quickly finalize the matter; if you choose not to do so—then I fear you must make a space journey."

"I don't have that much money," said Gersen. "Let me explain the circumstances—"

"No, I cannot reason with you; I have far to go and much to do. If you have no money, then you must act through the usual channels."

"Interchange?" asked Gersen with a wintry smile.

"Interchange. I wish you good fortune, Mr. Wall, or what-

ever your name; dealing with you has been a pleasure."
Seuman Otwal departed, and Gersen saw no more of him. He
was transferred to another ship, where he found himself in
the company of three children, two young women, three
older women, and a middle-aged man, presumably members
of various wealthy Concourse families. Time passed, how
long Gersen could not know. He ate and slept many times,
but at last the ship became still; there was the familiar but always unsettling wait as atmospheres equalized, then the
passengers were led out upon the soil of Sasani, ushered into
a bus, and conveyed across the desert to Interchange.

In a small auditorium, one of the Interchange functionaries
gave them a briefing. "Ladies and gentlemen, we are glad to
have you with us, and we hope that during your stay you will
try to rest, relax, and enjoy yourselves. The facilities of Interchange are those of a sanitarium; we allow a certain degree
of social intercourse, so long as decorum and courtesy is
maintained. We encourage the enjoyment of your special
hobbies and certain sports, such as swimming, chess, kalingo,
tennis, the use of musical instruments, and the chromatil.
There are no facilities for hiking, gliding, bird-watching,
marathon-running, or exploration of the fascinating Sasani
wilderness. We offer six classes of accommodation ranging
from hyper-luxurious Class AA to the standard E, which is
plain but by no means uncomfortable. The cuisine is of eight
standard categories, corresponding to the principal gastron-
omic habits of the Oikumene peoples. For persons who are
habituated to other more specialized diets, there is a special
service at extra charge. We flatter ourselves that anyone can
eat, if not with relish, at least with nourishment, at Interchange.

"Our regulations are somewhat more firm than those of the
average pleasure resort, and I must warn you that surrepti-
tious and solitary ventures across the desert can only lead to
inconvenience. In the first place, there are numerous carnivo-
rous insects. Secondly, there is neither food nor water.
Thirdly, the autochthonous inhabitants of Sasani, who leave
their burrows only at night, are anthropophages. Fourthly, we
are required to protect the interests of our clients, and the obstreperous individual (fortunately rare) soon finds himself deprived of all privileges."

"I will now distribute forms among you. Please indicate
your choice of accommodation and cuisine. You will notice a
list of regulations. Please read these carefully. You will find

the personnel courteous, if somewhat remote. They are well paid, so please do not attempt to press gratuities upon anyone. We regard this tendency with suspicion, and inquire carefully into the motives of those who offer such inducements."

"Tomorrow you will be provided with means of communication with those who might be expected to rescind your fees. That is all, and thank you."

Gersen examined the form, and selected Class B accommodations, which allowed him full use of the institution's recreational activities, as well as a modicum of privacy. He had eaten the food of all the Oikumene—including Sandusk, he thought wryly, recalling the shopkeeper of Ard Street—and indeed was not over-fastidious. He checked the category "classic," the cuisine of Alphanor, West Earth, and perhaps a third of the population of the Oikumene.

He read the "Regulations," none of which were surprising or ominous except Item 19: "Those persons who are in residence after their period of prime rescission and who thereupon fall into the 'Available' category, must keep to their apartments during the morning period in order to allow inspection by noncommitted visitors who might be interested in paying rescission fees."

In due course, Gersen was taken to his apartment, which seemed comfortable enough. The parlor contained a desk, a table, several chairs, a green and black rug, a shelf stacked with periodicals. The walls were mauve spattered with orange, the ceiling a foxy russet. The bathroom included the usual facilities, with walls, floor, and ceiling finished in seal-brown tile. The bed was narrow and austerely padded, the infra-radiator suspended obtrusively from the ceiling as in old-fashioned country inns.

Gersen bathed, dressed in the fresh garments provided, lay down on his bed, and considered the possible directions of the future. First, it was necessary to rid himself of the depression and self-deprecation that had been his mood since Seuman Otwal's white light had first flashed into his face. He had all too long considered himself invulnerable, protected by destiny—merely because of the force of his motivations. It was perhaps his single superstition: the sollipsistic conviction that, one after another, those five individuals who had destroyed Mount Pleasant must die at his hands. Persuaded by his faith, Gersen had neglected the commonsense act of killing Seuman Otwal—and had suffered the consequences.

He must rearrange his patterns of thinking. He had been complacent, doctrinaire, didactic in his approach. He had conducted himself as if the success of his ambitions were preordained; as if he were endowed with supernatural capacities. All quite wrong, Gersen told himself. Seuman Otwal had taken him with ridiculous ease. Seuman Otwal held him so cheap that he had not even bothered to question him, but had flung him into a hold with the rest of his bag. And Gersen's self-esteem was further mortified. He had not previously appreciated the full extent of his vanity. Very well then, he told himself: if absolute resourcefulness, absolute indomitability were the basic elements of his nature, it was now time to put these attributes to work.

Less angry—indeed, half-amused with his own earnestness he took stock of the situation. Tomorrow, if he so chose, he could notify Patch of his predicament. There was nothing to be gained by this. Gersen himself had the half-million paid him by Patch—originally money supplied by Duschane Audmar—and perhaps another seventy or eighty thousand from the money left him by his grandfather. His rescission fee was a million SVU more than this: a sum far beyond his ability to raise.

If Kokor Hekkus, or Seuman Otwal—the same man?— could be convinced that he and Patch had parted company, they might try to re-kidnap Patch and lower Gersen's fee to the money he had received from the sale of his partnership. But Patch, if he were wise, would take himself out of circulation. Gersen might be held at Interchange for months, or years. Eventually Interchange fees would begin to eat into the sponsor's profit; the rescission fee would drop. As soon as it reached half a million Gersen could buy his own way out—unless an independent purchaser considered him worth more: an unlikely circumstance.

In effect, Gersen was confined at Interchange for an indefinite period.

What of escape? Gersen had never heard of escape from Interchange. If a person managed to elude the vigilance of the guards and the careful system of alarms, tattletales, and trigger-beams, where could he go? The desert was fatal by day, even more so by night. Automatic weapons barred helpful spacecraft from the area. No one departed Interchange except through death or the rescission of their fees. It occurred to Gersen to wonder about Alusz Iphigenia Eperje-Tokay, the girl from Thamber. Her fee was ten billion SVU, a fantastic sum: how close had Kokor Hekkus come to paying it? How gratifying to rescind Alusz Iphigenia out from under the very nose of Kokor Hekkus! A visionary dream, when he could not rescind his own comparatively modest fee.

A gong sounded, to announce the evening meal. Gersen went to his designated dining area along the blank-walled walk topped with the tight interlacement of glass bands that characterized the avenues and walk-ways of Interchange. The dining room was a high-ceilinged room painted austerely gray. The guests ate at small individual tables and were served from carts passing back and forth. There was a penal-colony atmosphere to the dining room that was more or less absent from the rest of Interchange; Gersen could not define its source, unless it was the isolation of the diners, the lack of gossip or banter between the tables. The food was synthetic, of poor color, not too well prepared, in quantities not too generous. Even Gersen, who took no great interest in food, found the meal unappetizing. If this was Class B cuisine, he wondered what Class E was like. Perhaps not much different.

After dinner came the so-called social hour, in a large compound domed against the dusty Sasani night wind. Here the entire guest population of Interchange collected after the evening meal, from boredom and curiosity: who had come, who had gone? At the central kiosk, Gersen signed a chit for beer, carried the paper container to a bench, seated himself. Perhaps two hundred other people were in view: folk of all ages and races, some walking, a few playing chess, a few conversing, others like himself drinking morosely on the benches. There was no great gregariousness; everyone displayed near-identical expressions: flat dislike for Interchange and everything connected with it, including their fellow guests. Even the children seemed infected by the general gloom, though they showed a greater disposition to clot into groups. Perhaps twenty young women were in evidence, even more aloof, injured, and indignant than the rest. Gersen inspected them with curiosity: which was Alusz Iphigenia? If Kokor Hekkus were made to possess her, she must necessarily be extraordinarily beautiful; none here seemed to fulfill the requirements. Nearby, a tall girl with striking red hair gazed broodingly at her long fingers, each joint of which was banded with a black metal sleeve identifying her as an Eginand of Copus. Beyond, a small dark-skinned girl sipped wine; she seemed winsome and appealing, but not one who would think to value herself at ten billion SVU.

There were others, but all seemed too old or too young, or of no particular beauty—such as the young woman at the other end of his bench who might just conceivably fit the requirements. Her skin was pale, tinged with dusky ivory; she had clear gray eyes and regular features; her hair was tawny blonde: in short she was not unattractive but hardly in the ten billion SVU class. Gersen would not have considered her a second time had it not been for a certain insolent poise to her head, a certain cool intelligence of gaze. . . . But no, for all her clear eyes and regular features, she was too ordinary, too unexceptional. . . . The attendant who had served Gersen on his previous visit crossed the compound, looking neither right nor left. What was his name? Armand Koshiel. And Gersen became more morose than before. . . . The social period ended; the guests wandered away to their various suites, apartments, and rooms.

The morning meal—tea, muffins, and compote—was served directly in the apartment, after which Gersen was summoned to the central administration building, where he found himself in the company of several of the persons with whom he had come to Interchange.

Presently his name was called. He entered the office of a harried-looking clerk, who gave him a perfunctory salute, and delivered a well-rehearsed speech: "Mr. Wall, seat yourself, if you will. From your point of view your presence here is a misfortune; from ours, you are a guest to be treated with courtesy and dignity. We are anxious to improve the light in which we are regarded; we will take all practical means to that end. Now you are here sponsored by Mr. Kokor Hekkus. His demand is for the sum of SVU 1,681,490, and I now inquire how you propose to secure this sum." He waited expectantly.

"I wish I knew," said Gersen. "It is totally unrealistic."

The official nodded. "Many of our guests find their fees excessive. As you know, we have no control over the fees demanded; we can only advise the sponsor to moderation, and the guest to a cooperative attitude. Now then—can you raise this sum?"

"No."

"What of your family?"

"Nonexistent."

"Friends?"

"I have no friends."

"Business associates?"

"None."

The clerk sighed. "Then you must remain here until one of these events occurs: the sponsor may lower his demands to a feasible sum. Fifteen days after the date your associates have first had opportunity to appear in your behalf you go on an 'available' basis, and the sponsorship fee may be paid by anyone, who then receives you into custody. After a certain period, unless board and room bills are regularly met, we may be forced to release custody to a noncommitted visitor for the extent of these bills. So then?"

"I can't meet the figure. I have no one to notify."

"We will state as much to your sponsor. Do you care to name the maximum figure you can pay?"

"About half a million," said Gersen reluctantly.

"I will so inform your sponsor. In the meantime, Mr. Wall, I trust that you find your visit not too unpleasant."

"Thank you."

Gersen was conducted back to his apartment, and presently released to the dining room for lunch.

During the afternoon, the recreational facilities of Interchange were made free to him. There were minor sports, crafts, games; he could exercise at a gymnasium, swim in a pool. Or he could remain in his apartment. Visiting the apartment or room of another guest was forbidden.

Several days passed. Gersen became tense and charged with the need for activity. There was no scope to release this pressure except in exercise at the gymnasium. He pondered escape. It seemed impossible; there was no place to start.

During the social hour of the third day, Gersen, turning away from the kiosk with beer came face to face with Armand Koshiel, whose schedule apparently brought him through the compound-at about this time. Koshiel murmured a polite apology, stepped aside; then turned a puzzled glance backward.

Gersen grinned ruefully. "Conditions have altered since our last meeting."

"So I see," said Koshiel. "I remember you well. It's Mr. Gassoon? Mr. Grisson?"

"Wall," said Gersen. "Howard Wall."

"Of course: Mr. Wall." Koshiel shook his head in bemused wonder. "Isn't it strange the way fate works? But now, sir, I must be off. We aren't allowed to chat with the guests."

"Tell me something. How close to ten billion SVU has Kokor Hekkus achieved?"

"He progresses, he approaches, so I understand. All of us here are interested; it's the largest fee ever to be rescinded."

Gersen felt an irrational pang of anger—or perhaps jealousy. "Does the woman come down to the compound?"

"I have seen her here on occasion." Koshiel made tentative efforts to sidle away.

"What does she look like?"

Koshiel knit his brows, glanced furtively over his shoulder. "She's by no means what you might expect. Not a clever jolly type, if you know what I mean. Please excuse me, Mr. Wall, I must be off, or face reprimand."

Gersen went to his usual bench, seething with a new set of dissatisfactions. This unknown woman, by all logical processes, should mean nothing to him. . . . Such was not the case. Gersen puzzled over himself and his motives. How and why had he become fascinated? Because of Alusz Iphigenia's self-appraised value of ten billion SVU? The fact that Kokor Hekkus, in all his egotism and arrogance, was about to possess her? (The thought awoke a peculiar fury in him.) Because of her asserted origin: mythical Thamber? Because of the stirrings of his own sternly repressed romanticism? Whatever the cause, Gersen scrutinized the compound seeking the beautiful girl who might be Alusz Iphigenia of Thamber. She definitely was not the small dark girl, nor the red-haired Eginand from Copus. The tawny-blonde girl with the withdrawn manner was not in evidence, but she hardly qualified. Though, Gersen reflected, her eyes were an exceedingly lucent grey and no exception could be taken to her figure, which was rather slight and delicate, but perfectly proportioned. The gong sounded; he returned to his apartment disappointed and roiling with uneasiness.

The next day passed; Gersen waited impatiently for the social period. It finally arrived; a new woman was present. She was lithe and supple, with long legs, a long patrician face, a dazzling roll of bright white hair, intricately coiffed. Gersen inspected her carefully. No, he decided with a feeling of relief; this could not be Alusz Iphigenia of Thamber; this woman was too intricate, too artificial. She might well value herself at ten billion SVU, and Gersen was almost willing that Kokor Hekkus should pay such an amount and take possession. The tawny-blonde girl did not appear. Gersen returned to his apartment in disgust and vexation. While he was pent and helpless, Kokor Hekkus was easing in upon his quarry. To distract himself, Gersen read old magazines until midnight.

The following day was like those previous: they began to merge, lose identity. At lunch there were two new members to his group. Gersen overheard a comment that identified the newcomers as Tychus Hasselberg, First Chairman of the Jarnell Corporation, and Skerde Vorek, Director of Forestlands, both of Earth, both millionaires several hundred times over. Two steps closer to the goal, thought Gersen sourly.

During the afternoon he exercised in the gymnasium. At dinner the food seemed more than ordinarily tasteless. Gersen went to the "social hour" in a surly mood. He provided himself a mug of musty Sasani wine, and seated himself in expectation of another dreary evening. Half an hour passed, then at the entrance to the compound appeared the tawnyblonde girl. Tonight she seemed even more abstracted than on the former occasion. Gersen watched her intently: actually, he thought, she was really not plain. Her features were so perfect, so perfectly placed as to make her face seem unremarkable—but certainly she was not plain. He watched her procure a mug of tea at the central kiosk; then she came to sit on a bench not far from Gersen. He studied her with great interest, his pulse moving rather swiftly. Why? he asked himself in irritation. Why did this young woman, at best conventionally attractive, affect him to such an extent?

He rose, walked to where she sat. "May I join you?" he asked.

"If you care to," she said after just sufficient hesitation to indicate that she'd rather sit quietly by herself. Her voice had a pleasant archaic swing, and Gersen tried to place her accent. "Excuse me for being curious," he said, "but are you Alusz Iphigenia Eperje-Tokay?"

"I am Alusz Iphigenia Eperje-Tokay," she said, correcting his pronunciation.

Gersen drew a deep breath. His instinct had been correct! From close at hand, and looking into her face, her quiet good looks seemed somewhat less quiet. She might almost be termed handsome. It was her eyes, he thought, that gave life to her face. Beauty? Sufficient to urge Kokor Hekkus to such flamboyant exertions? It seemed unlikely. "And your home is on the planet Thamber?"

She turned him another brief incurious look. "Yes."

"Do you know that to most people Thamber is an imaginary world, a place of legend and ballad?"

"So I have learned, to my surprise. I assure you it is far from imaginary." She sipped her tea, gave Gersen another swift glance. Her eyes, large, clear, candid, were her best feature, and these were undoubtedly beautiful. But now, a subtle shift in her position indicated disinterest in further conversation.

"I wouldn't bother you," said Gersen stiffly, "except for the fact that your fiancé Kokor Hekkus has brought me here, and I regard him as my enemy."

Alusz Iphigenia reflected a moment. "You act unwisely in regarding him as an enemy."

"Suppose he rescinds your fee, what then?"

She shrugged. "It is a matter I do not care to discuss." Gersen thought, yes, she is beyond doubt handsome; even more than handsome: when she spoke, even when she thought, her features took on a luminosity, a vitality that transfigured even ordinary features.

Gersen was at a loss for a means to continue the conversation. Finally he asked, "Do you know Kokor Hekkus well?"

"Not well. He keeps for the most part to Misk, the Land Beyond the Mountains. My home is Draszane in Gentilly."

"How were you able to come here? Do many spaceships come to Thamber?"

"No." She turned him a sudden sharp glance. "Who are you? Are you one of his spies?"

Gersen shook his head. Looking into her face, he thought with amazement, *Did I ever think this girl plain? She is beautiful, inexpressibly so.* He said, "If I were free, I could help you."

She laughed, rather cruelly. "How can you help me, when you can't even help yourself?" And Gersen felt an unfamiliar red flush seep across his face. He rose to his feet. "Good night."

Alusz Iphigenia said nothing; Gersen stalked off to his apartment. He showered and threw himself on his bed. Suppose he communicated with Duschane Audmar? Pointless; Audmar would not even bother to send him a refusal. Myron Patch? More than pointless. Ben Zaum? He might be able to raise five or ten thousand SVU, no more. . . . Gersen picked up one of the old magazines, flicked through the pages. . . . A face looked forth, one which he seemed to recognize. Gersen glanced down at the caption. The name, Daeniel Trembath, was unknown to him. . . . Strange, Gersen flipped the page. The face was extremely like that of—of whom? Gersen turned back to the face. He had known this man as 'Mr. Hoskins'; he had brought back his corpse from Bissom's End. Gersen read the caption in full:

> Daeniel Trembath, Arch-Director of the Bank of Rigel, now retiring. Fifty-one years his Excellency the Director has served the great bank and the peoples of the Concourse; last week he announced his retirement. What are his future plans? "I will rest. I have worked hard and long; perhaps too hard and too long. Now I will take time to enjoy the aspects of life denied me by my responsibilities."

Gersen looked at the date of the magazine. It was *Cosmopolis* for January, 1525. Three months later Trembath disappeared; a week or so afterwards he was dead, by the act of Billy Windle—who might be Kokor Hekkus—on an unpleasant little world Beyond. Gersen, now wide awake, thought back across the months. Why would the retired Arch-Director of the great Bank of Rigel travel so remotely, so secretly to deal with the man who called himself Billy Windle? Trembath had wanted perpetual youth: what did he have to offer in exchange? By the very nature of his career, it could be nothing but money. The meeting at Skouse had occurred immediately after Alusz Iphigenia had taken sanctuary at Interchange; the concatenation of places, events, and personalities was intriguing. Kokor Hekkus wanted money— ten billion SVU. Daeniel Trembath, Arch-Director (retired) of the Bank of Rigel, was the very symbol of money—and also conservative respectability. Why had the IPCC wanted his return, dead or alive? Surely Trembath had not stolen ten billion SVU? Gersen remembered the fragment of paper he had taken from Mr. Hoskins at Skouse. He strove to recall the words, now suddenly so pregnant with possibility:

> —crimps, or more properly, bands of density. These apparently occur at random, though in practice they are so casual as to be imperceptible. The critical spacing is in terms of the square root of the first eleven primes. The occurrence of six or more such crimps at any of the designated locations will validate—

The conclusions to be drawn were staggering. There was likewise an aspect to the situation that was the very soul of tragi-comedy. Gersen jumped to his feet, paced back and forth across his apartment. If circumstances were as he suspected, how could he take advantage of his knowledge?

He thought for an hour, formulating and discarding various schemes. The crafts and hobby shop seemed the key to the situation. The activities encouraged would be simple and easily supervised: wood-carving, puppetry, embroidery, shawl-weaving, water-colors, glass-melting. Possibly photography. . . . The morning passed with a dismal slowness. Gersen sat sprawled in the most comfortable of his chairs. A delightful variation to his scheme occurred to him; he laughed aloud. . . . Immediately after lunch, he visited the hobby room. It was more or less as he had expected: a large room equipped with looms, pots of modeling clay, paints, beads, wire, various other paraphernalia. The attendant in charge was a corpulent man of early middle-age, bald, with small doll-like features in a round face. He answered Gersen's questions with a reasonable degree of patience. No; there were no facilities for photographic work. Several years ago an effort had been made in this direction, but the project had been abandoned: the equipment required too much maintenance had occupied too much of his time. Gersen put forward a delicately phrased proposal: He, Gersen, was almost certain to be a guest for a month or perhaps two; prior to his coming he had been experimenting with certain novel art-forms involving photography, and he wished to continue his activities—to such an extent that he would be willing to purchase the necessary equipment.

The attendant considered, with a wet pursing of the mouth. The project seemed to entail a great deal of trouble—for Gersen, for himself, for everyone involved. In theory, of course, it was conceivable, but—he gave an eloquent shrug of the shoulders. Gersen uttered a reassuring laugh: any extra attention on the attendant's part—what was his name? Funian Lubby—would be adequately, or even, Gersen amended cautiously, generously rewarded. Lubby sighed heavily. Interchange policy dictated full cooperation with the guests, within understandable limits. If Mr. Wall insisted, Lubby could only do as he required. As to the remuneration Mr. Wall had suggested, it was against Interchange policy, but Mr. Wall must be the judge of what was right. How soon could Lubby provide the proper equipment? asked Gersen. If Mr. Wall provided a list and the necessary funds, an order could be placed at Sagbad, the largest nearby trade center:

delivery could be expected tomorrow at the earliest; more likely the day following.

Excellent, said Gersen. He seated himself, wrote out a list. It was long, and included a number of items intended to obscure Gersen's primary purpose. Lubby pursed his lips hugely, in surprise and automatic disapprobation. Gersen said hurriedly, "I realize that this makes enormous inconvenience for you: is a hundred SVU sufficient compensation for your extra effort?"

"You understand," said Lubby sternly, "that regulations forbid the transfer of funds between guests and personnel. In a case of this sort, the money involved is merely a means of providing the craft shop with sorely needed equipment—since I presume you will leave these items here on your departure?"

Gersen did not wish to seem too eager. "I suppose so. Some of them at least—those that duplicate my own equipment at home." All in all, he was highly encouraged. That Lubby could speak so openly indicated that the craft shop was not under remote surveillance. "What do you think this material and equipment will cost?" he inquired.

Lubby appraised the list. "Megaphot camera . . . Chago enlarger and printer . . . Ball microscope. Expensive items all. . . . Tanglemat duplicator. . . . What would you be needing that for?"

"I prepare kaleidoscopic permutations of natural objects," said Gersen. "Sometimes twenty or thirty copies of a single print are needed, and I find the duplicator convenient."

"It will cost a fortune," grumbled Funian Lubby, "but if you're willing to pay for it—"

"Yes, if I must," said Gersen. "I dislike spending money, but I like two months away from my hobby even less."

"Understandable." Lubby glanced down the list. "This is an impressive list of chemicals. I hope," he said with a sardonic twist of the lips, "that you are not planning to blow up the institution, and thus destroy my livelihood."

Gersen laughed at the joke. "I'm sure you are sufficiently knowledgeable to forestall anything of this nature. No, there are no explosives, corrosives, or noxious substances here: only inks, dyes, photo-sensitives, and the like."

"So I see. I am by no means uninformed in these matters. I am an accredited Scientific Academician of Boomaraw College on Lorgan, and in fact have done research on the flatfish of the Neuster Ocean, until my appointment was canceled—another regressive trick of the Institute, of that I am sure."

"Yes, a sad situation," Gersen agreed. "A person wonders where it will end. Do they want to make cavemen of us all?"

"Who knows what the wretched malcontents hope for? I have heard that they are slowly acquiring control of the Jarnel Corporation, that when they finally secure their 51 percent—then *pfui*! no more spaceships, no more travel. What will that do to us? Where will that leave me? Without a job, if I am so unfortunate as still to be alive. No, I spit on those people."

Gersen had been inspecting the craft room. "Where can I work to be the least obtrusive? Preferably in some corner where I can throw up a screen to keep out the light. Naturally any effort on your part I am willing to pay for; indeed if there were a dis-used store-room, or something of the sort. . . ."

"Yes." Funian Lubby heaved himself to his feet. "Let us look. The old sculpting studio is no longer in use; guests nowadays care nothing for serious work."

The studio was octagonal, the walls were native wood varnished a sour brown; the floor was stained yellow brick, the ceiling rose to a skylight through which came a grayish, almost mauve, illumination. "I'll block out the light," said Gersen. "Otherwise the room is quite suitable." To test the degree of freedom from surveillance he said, "Now I understand that the rules forbid the exchange of money between guests and personnel, still rules are made to be broken, and it is not fair that you should go to extra exertion without reimbursement. You agree?"

"I think you have expressed my point of view exactly."

"Good. What goes on in this old studio then concerns no one but you and me. While I am not a wealthy man, I am not parisimonious, and I am willing to pay for my pleasures." He brought forth his checkbook, wrote a draft for 3,000 SVU upon the Bank of Rigel. "This should pay for all the items of my list and leave enough to compensate you."

Lubby puffed out his cheeks. "That should do very nicely. I will give your order special attention, and who knows? the equipment may be here tomorrow."

Gersen went away well satisfied. His hopes might be based on a set of false premises—but checking and rechecking, he felt secure. How could it be otherwise?

But he needed one more item, the most important of all.

This job he dared not entrust to Funian Lubby, except as a last resort. He made out another draft for twenty thousand SVU, tucked it into his pocket.

That night, Alusz Iphigenia made no appearance at the social hour. Gersen did not care. He walked slowly back and forth, watching, waiting, and then just as he was about to give up hope, Armand Koshiel appeared, taking a shortcut through the compound. Gersen approached him as casually as possible. "I am going to walk past the waste-paper bin," he said. "I will drop a scrap of paper. Come behind me, pick it up. You will find a draft for twenty thousand SVU. Get me a ten thousand SVU note on the Bank of Rigel. Keep the remaining ten thousand." Without waiting for a reply he turned away, sauntered toward the kiosk. From the corner of his eye he saw Koshiel give a slight shrug, then continue the way he was going.

At the kiosk, Gersen bought a sack of sweets. Pausing at the waste-paper bin he tossed aside the sack into which he had tucked the bank draft, and crossing to a bench seated himself.

The crumpled bit of paper beside the bin looked large, white, and conspicuous. Here came Koshiel back across the compound. He went to the kiosk, spoke a jocular word to the attendant, selected a bag of sweets for himself, tossed the paper toward the bin. He bent after it, picked up Gersen's bag, seemed to drop them both into the bin, and walked away.

Gersen went to his apartment, nerves tingling. His scheme had been set into motion. Too much optimism would be foolish, but so far all went well. A hidden monitor might have observed Koshiel pick up the bank draft; Funian Lubby might impose too much supervision upon him, or so much new equipment might attract the attention of persons less genial than Lubby. Still—so far, so good.

The following day he looked briefly into the crafts room. Lubby was occupied with a pair of children who in their boredom had turned to mask-making. The equipment would not be delivered until the morrow, said Lubby, and Gersen departed.

The evening social hour passed with neither Koshiel nor Alusz Iphigenia making an appearance. On the following day, when Gersen returned to his apartment after breakfast he found an envelope on his desk containing a green and pink SVU 10,000 bank note. Gersen tested it with his fake-meter, which, with a few other personal effects, he had been allowed to keep. The meter gave a satisfactory acknowledgment. So far, so good. Gersen dared make no further experiments; he might even then be under scrutiny. So far, so good. But his equipment still had not arrived, and Funian Lubby seemed in a bad mood; Gersen returned to his apartment seething with impatience. Never had a day passed so slowly, though fortunately the Sasani day was only twenty-one hours long.

On the afternoon following, Funian Lubby indicated a set of cartons with an affable wave of his fat hand. "There you are, Mr. Wall. A fine set of equipment, and you can go about your prisms or kaleidoscopes, whatever it is you do, with all your might."

"Thank you, Mr. Lubby, I'm very pleased," said Gersen. He carried the cartons into the old sculpting studio, and with Lubby assisting and crooning in pleasure, unpacked them.

"I'm anxious to see your work," said Lubby. "One can always learn, and this is a creative technique I have never observed before."

"It's a very detailed process," said Gersen. "Some people even find it tedious, but I enjoy slow careful work. The first step, I think, is to close off the skylight and light-seal the door."

With Lubby steadying the ladder, Gersen stapled opaque cloth across the skylight, then prepared a sign that read: *Photographic Darkroom—Knock before Entering*, and attached it to the door. "Now," he said, "I'm ready to begin." He considered. "I think I'll start with a simple reiteration in green and pink."

With Lubby watching with vast interest, Gersen solemnly photographed a pin, enlarged it ten diameters, prepared a master copy from which he printed thirty copies in green and thirty in pink on the autolith.

"What next?" asked Lubby.

"Now we come to the painstaking part of the job. Each of these pins must be carefully cut from the background. Then with pins and pin-shaped holes, I create the reiteration. If you desire you may do the cutting while I formulate the correct color of ink."

Lubby looked dubiously at the stack of prints. "All these are to be cut out?"

"Yes; very carefully."

Lubby unenthusiastically set to work. Gersen watched closely, giving advice and stressing the need for absolute accuracy. Then, borrowing Lubby's slide-rule, he calculated the square root of the first eleven prime numbers: values ranging from 1 to 4.79. Lubby meanwhile had cut out three pins, making a single small mistake. Gersen complained aggrievedly. Lubby put down the scissors. "This is extremely interesting, but I fear I must look to other matters."

As soon as he had gone, Gersen compared the 10,000 SVU bank note with the pink and green pins, adjusted the colors, added a mordant and a catalyst, and printed further pins.

He glanced into the outer studio; Lubby was busy with the children. Gersen took the note to the microscope, and—as so many of thousands had done before him—examined it with an eye to discovering the secret of its authenticity. Like the thousands before him, he discovered no such quality. Now—the key experiment, upon which the success of the entire project depended. He selected paper of density and weight similar to the bank note, cut a rectangle to the size of the note: precisely five by two and a quarter inches. He passed the paper through the fake-meter: the alarm-light glowed, now Gersen laid off points along the length of the paper rectangle corresponding to the square roots he had computed. Next he laid a straight-edge across the paper and at each pair of points scored a cross mark with the point of a nail—thus, so he hoped 'crimping' and 'compressing' the fibers. With trembling fingers he lifted the fake-meter. . . . The door opened; into the room came Funian Lubby. With one motion Gersen slid fake-meter, bank note, and paper rectangle into his pocket; with another, he picked up scissors and prints, simulated intent creativity. Lubby was disappointed to find that with so much equipment so little had been produced. He expressed himself to this effect; Gersen explained that he had been recalculating certain aesthetic laws: a tedious process. If Lubby so desired, he could expedite the process by cutting out more pins, very carefully. Lubby declared himself unable to be of further assistance. Gersen cut out a few of the pins while Lubby watched, arranged them with extreme care on the table-top. Lubby looked over the pink and green test panels that Gersen had set under a lamp. "Are these the only two colors you will use?"

"At least for this present composition," said Gersen. "Pink and green, though they might seem somewhat obvious or even naïve, are for my purposes absolutely essential."

Lubby grunted. "They appear particularly bland: even faded."

"True," said Gersen. "I have added certain agents to the pigments; it appears that the light tends to bleach them."

Lubby presently returned to the main room. Gersen brought forth his fake-meter, passed the paper rectangle into the slot. No red light, but rather the heart-warming buzz of authenticity: the most musical sound of Gersen's existence.

He looked at his watch: the period was almost at an end. There was no time for further work.

At the social hour, Alusz Iphigenia made an appearance, to stand aloofly at the back of the compound. Gersen made no attempt to approach her, and, so far as he could tell, she seemed indifferent to his existence. . . . He had thought her plain! He had considered her features uninteresting! They were perfect; she was the most entrancing thing he had ever seen. Ten billion SVU? A pittance! He could almost applaud Kokor Hekkus' discrimination. . . . Gersen could hardly wait to return to the craft shop.

But the following afternoon found Funian Lubby at his most tiresome. There were no other hobbyists present, and for two hours Lubby sat gaping with eyes protuberant and fascinated as Gersen cut paper pins, arranged and rearranged them with frowning concentration, his whole soul aching with the wish that Lubby depart.

The day was wasted; Gersen left the shop seething with suppressed fury.

The following day he fared better. Lubby was busy. Gersen photographed the bank note with serial number masked, printed two hundred copies with carefully prepared inks. The day after, on the pretext of exposing large areas of photo-sensitive paper, he locked the door. Then, contriving a jig, he crimped the new notes, and using a toy printing press, printed new serial numbers. The notes looked about the same as the genuine; they had a somewhat different feel—but what matter? They satisfied the fake-meter.

As Gersen ate dinner he pondered his final problem: how to rescind his fees without arousing suspicion. If he merely presented himself at the office, the question would be raised as to how the money had come into his possession. . . . He could think of no practical or feasible means to have a parcel delivered to him. Certainly he could not trust Koshiel with so much money.

He decided that he needed more information. During the social hour, he went to the office of the assistant ordinator, a weasel-faced man wearing the dark blue Interchange uniform as if it were a privilege. Gersen put on a face of worry. "I have something of a problem," he told the ordinator. "It has been reported to me that an old friend is coming here tomorrow to rescind one of the guests. Can it be arranged that I look into the bureau when the bus arrives from the spaceport?"

The ordinator frowned. "This is a somewhat irregular request."

"I realize this," said Gersen, "however Interchange policy is to facilitate the rescission of fees, and such is the case here."

"Very well," said the ordinator. "Be here at this office tomorrow immediately after the morning meal, and I will arrange the matter."

Gersen went to the compound, paced back and forth, drank quantities of wine to quiet his nerves. The night passed; he choked down a few bites of breakfast, hurried to the office of the ordinator, who pretended to have forgotten the arrangement. Gersen patiently restated his case.

"Oh, very well," said the ordinator. "I suppose we can't expect every rescission to work through the proper channels." He conducted Gersen to an antechamber of the reception room. Here they waited.

The archaic old bus arrived, discharged eight passengers. They filed into the reception room.

"Well?" asked the ordinator. "Is one of these your friend?"

"Yes indeed," said Gersen. "That short man with the blue skin-tone. I'll just speak a word or two to him and arrange my rescission." Before the ordinator could object, Gersen went out into the reception room, approached the man he had designated. "Excuse me; aren't you Myron Patch of Patris?"

"No sir. I am no such individual."

"My mistake." Gersen returned to the ordinator, carrying an envelope. "Everything is well. He has brought my money. I am a free man."

The ordinator grunted. The event seemed rather peculiar—but weren't peculiar events part of life? "Your friend came to rescind you and someone else also?"

"Yes. He is a member of the Institute and doesn't care to display too much cordiality."

The ordinator grunted again. All was explained—at least, all seemed to be explained. "Very well," he said, "if you have your money, go rescind yourself. I'll say a word to the clerk, since the process is somewhat irregular."

When the bus departed Interchange, Gersen was aboard. At Nichae he hired an air-car and was taken to the city Sagbad.

Five days later, wearing black skin-tone, black and brown tunic with black breeches, Gersen returned to Interchange aboard the antique bus. He went into the now-familiar office, submitted to the officiousness of the clerk. "And whom do you wish to rescind?"

"Alusz Iphigenia Eperje-Tokay."

The clerk's eyebrows rose. "You, sir, are Kokor Hekkus?" He spoke with awe.

"No."

The clerk made nervous movements. "The fee is large. Ten billion SVU."

Gersen opened the flat black case he was carrying, withdrew packets of bank notes in 100,000 SVU denominations: the largest in circulation. "Here is the money."

"Yes, yes. . . . But—well, I must inform you that Kokor Hekkus has already deposited with us over nine billion SVU."

"Here is ten billion. Count it."

The clerk made a flustered sound. "You are within your rights. The guest is admittedly 'available.' " With trembling fingers he touched the money. "I will need help to count so much money."

Counting and fake-metering the money occupied six men four hours. The clerk signed a receipt with a nervous flourish. "Very well, sir, here you are. I will send for the guest whose fees you have rescinded. She will be here at once." And he muttered under his breath: "Kokor Hekkus will not enjoy this. Someone will suffer."

Ten minutes later Alusz Iphigenia arrived at the office. Her face was strained and wild; her eyes were bright with fear. She stared at Gersen without recognizing him; then went to the door as if to run out across the desert. Gersen restrained her. "Calm yourself," he told her. "I am not Kokor Hekkus; I have no designs upon you: consider yourself safe."

She looked at him incredulously, looked again, and now Gersen thought she recognized him.

"There is another matter," said the clerk. He addressed Alusz Iphigenia. "Since you are acting in the peculiar capacity of your own sponsor, the money, minus our 12½ percent fee, is yours."

Alusz Iphigenia stared at him apparently without comprehension. "I suggest," said Gersen, "that you prepare a bank draft, so that she need not carry around so much negotiable currency."

There was a flurry of consultation, a shrugging of shoulders, a flutter of hands; finally the bank draft was drawn upon the Planetary Bank of Sasani at Sagbad, in the sum of SVU 8,749,993,581: ten billion minus 12½ percent, minus charges of SVU 6,419 for special AA accommodation.

Gersen scrutinized the document with suspicion. "Presumably this is a valid draft? You have funds to cover?"

"Naturally," declared the official. "Indeed, Kokor Hekkus has deposited to our account a sum appreciably in excess of this amount."

"Very well," said Gersen, "this is acceptable." He turned to Alusz Iphigenia. "Come. The bus is waiting."

Still she hesitated, looking right and left as if again contemplating flight across the Da'ar-Rizm. But now one of the flying black insects struck her, clung to her arm; she brushed it off with a cry of fear.

"Come," said Gersen once again. "You can have either Kokor Hekkus, the insects, or me; and I will neither violate you or eat you alive."

Without further protest, she followed him to the bus. It lurched, roared, rumbled: Interchange became a white and gray tumble dimly glimpsed through the dust.

They sat side by side in the lurching bus. Then Alusz turned a puzzled sidelong glance at Gersen. "Who are you?"

"No friend of Kokor Hekkus."

"What are—what are you going to do with me?"

"Nothing discreditable."

"Where are we going then? You don't understand the nature of Kokor Hekkus; he will track us to the corners of the galaxy."

Gersen had no comment to make; the conversation came to an end. In truth Gersen felt none too secure; they were still vulnerable to interception. But the journey across the barrens passed without incident.

The bus bounced into Sul Arsam; they boarded the waiting air-ship and presently came down at the Nichae spaceport. To the side stood the sleek new Armintor Starskip Gersen had bought in Sagbad. Alusz Iphigenia hesitated before she went aboard, then gave a fatalistic shrug.

In Sagbad, there was a further delay at the Planetary Bank. Interchange provided a hesitant and worried verification, sensing something incorrect, yet at a loss to discover where. The chairman of the Planetary Bank reluctantly told Gersen, "Through a set of extraordinary circumstances, we have the sum in our vaults, representing a set of large deposits from Interchange. They are in notes of various denominations—"

"No matter; we will accept your count," said Gersen.

The money, Kokor Hekkus' laboriously accumulated hoard, was packed into four cases, carried out into the hired air-car.

Now the Head Cashier came running out into the area. "A communication from Interchange! For Mr. Wall!"

Gersen controlled his impulse to flee. He returned into the bank. On the visiphone screen appeared the face of the Director; behind stood a man Gersen did not recognize.

"Mr. Wall," said the Director, "there have been difficulties: this is Achill Gogan, representing Kokor Hekkus. He earnestly desires that you wait at Sagbad until he is able to confer with you."

"Certainly," said Gersen. "He may look for us at the Alamut Hotel."

Gersen departed the bank, entered the air-car where Alusz Iphigenia waited despondently with the money. "To the spaceport," he told the pilot.

Twenty minutes later Sasani lay behind them; engaging the intersplit, Gersen finally felt secure. The relief was intoxicating. He sat down on a settee and began to laugh. Alusz Iphigenia, across the cabin, watched with guarded interest. "Why do you laugh?"

"Because of how we were rescinded."

" 'We?' "

So she had not recognized him after all. Gersen came slowly across the cabin, and she moved back a distrustful half-inch. "One evening I spoke to you in the compound," said Gersen.

She studied him. "Now I remember you. The quiet man who sits in the shadows. How did you find so much money?"

"I printed it myself—and this is what amuses me."

She stared at him in bewilderment. "But they tested it! They accepted it!"

"Exactly. But here is the greatest joke of all: there is bleach in the ink. In a week they will have nothing. The money I paid Kokor Hekkus will be blank paper; the ten billion SVU will be blank paper. I have swindled Kokor Hekkus! I have swindled Interchange! Look: there is Kokor Hekkus' money!"

Alusz Iphigenia considered him dispassionately, then turned to look back toward Sasani. She smiled: a pensive smile. "Kokor Hekkus will be angry. No man alive has such extravagant emotions as Kokor Hekkus." She gave Gersen a look of something like wonder. "He would spend ten billion to gain me—because I chose to make this my price. And after he bought me—" she shuddered, "—he would derive ten billion SVU worth of use from me, by one means or another. When he gets you what he will do—is unthinkable."

"Unless I kill him first."

"You will find it difficult. Sion Trumble is the cleverest war chief of Thamber, and he has failed."

Gersen went to the galley, brought back a bottle of wine with two goblets. Alusz Iphigenia first made a negative motion, then thought better of it, and accepted the goblet. Gersen asked, "Do you know why I rescinded you?"

"No." But she fidgeted uncomfortably and a slow pink flush came into her face. Never, thought Gersen, had she seemed more beautiful. "Because you can guide me to Thamber, where I will find Kokor Hekkus and kill him."

The pink flush slowly subsided. She tasted the wine, gazed reflectively into the goblet. "I do not want to return to Thamber. I desperately fear Kokor Hekkus. He will now be insane with anger."

"Nevertheless, that is where we must go."

She shook her head pensively. "I cannot help you. Where Thamber lies I do not know."

CHAPTER 9

The captured revolutionary Tedoro exhorts his fellow prisoners:

> Allow nothing! Yield not so much as a quarter-inch! Eat the food they give you, concede no more! Who are they but villains? Shame them! Defy them! Hesitation is a crack in the steel; do you want them to bend you this way and that and snap you in two? Give nothing, yield nothing! If the commandant permits that you may sit, prefer to stand! If he gives you lined paper on which to write, write across the lines!

Gersen stared at Alusz Iphigenia incredulously. Then he jumped up to the control deck, disengaged the intersplit. The fabric of the ship exuded its almost human sigh of shock; the skin seemed to twitch along their bodies.

Motors dead, the Armintor Starskip drifted free in space. Aquila GB 1202 shone far astern, teetering at the edge of the psychological distinction between sun and star.

Gersen went into the head, showered away the black skintone, dressed in his usual space-garb: shorts, sandals, a light singlet. He returned to the saloon to find Alusz Iphigenia sitting where he had left her, gazing at the floor.

Gersen said nothing, but seated himself on the bench opposite, thoughtfully sipped his wine. Finally she spoke. "Why did you turn off the engines?"

"There is no point traveling at random. Since we have no destination we might as well remain here."

She shrugged, scowled. "Keep the money; take me to Earth. I have no wish to hang foolishly out here in space."

Gersen shook his head. "I rescinded your fee at great risk to myself—primarily to learn the whereabouts of Thamber. Secondarily, I find you attractive as a woman. I agree with Kokor Hekkus: you are worth ten billion SVU."

Alusz Iphigenia said angrily, "You do not believe me! It is

110

a fact: I could not return to Thamber if it were the dearest wish of my life!"

"How did you leave?"

"Sion Trumble captured a small spaceboat in a raid on Omad Island, which is Kokor Hekkus' spaceport. I read the Operator's Manual, and it seemed simple enough. When Kokor Hekkus threatened war on Gentilly unless my father gave me to him, I had two choices. I could kill myself or I could leave Thamber. I left. In the ship there was a Handbook of the Planets. It mentioned Sasani and described Interchange as the only locality in the human universe safe from criminals."

She turned a scathing glance toward Gersen. "This is inaccurate. Interchange apparently is fair game for counterfeiters."

Gersen acknowledged the fact with a grin and by refilling his wine glass. He hesitated before drinking it: the bottle had been left alone in the cabin while he showered: not inconceivably the woman had poisoned it. He put the glass aside. "And who is Sion Trumble?"

"The Prince of Vadrus, on the western border of Misk. We were to have been betrothed. . . . He is a brave warrior, and has done many noteworthy deeds."

"I see." Gersen ruminated. "Don't you know the way you came, from Thamber to Sasani?"

"I set the astrogation dials for Sasani, and left Thamber behind. I know only this and no more. Kokor Hekkus is the only man of Thamber to own a spaceship."

"What is the name of your sun?"

"Just 'Sun.' "

"Is it somewhat orange?"

"Yes. How did you know?"

"Deduction. What does the night sky look like? Are there any unusual objects in the sky? Any nearby double or triple stars?"

"No. Nothing unusual."

"Have there been any recent novae nearby?"

"What are 'novae?' "

"Stars suddenly exploding to give off great amounts of light."

"No, nothing like that."

"What of the Milky Way? Do you see it as a band around the sky, as a cloud, or how?"

"A ribbon of light streams across the night sky during winter: is that what you mean?"

"Yes. Apparently you're out toward the fringes."

"That may be." Alusz Iphigenia was unenthusiastic.

"What about tradition?" asked Gersen. "Are there old tales of Earth, or any of the other worlds?"

"Nothing very definite. . . . A few legends, a few old songs." She regarded him with an expression that seemed faintly derisive. "How is it that your *Star Directory* and your *Handbook to the Planets* can't tell you what you want to know?"

"Thamber is a lost world. Whoever ruled Thamber in the ancient days kept the secret well. There's no information now—except a nursery rhyme:

> Set a course from the old Dog Star
> A point to the north of Achernar;
> Sleight your ship to the verge extreme
> And dead ahead shines Thamber's gleam.

Alusz Iphigenia smiled faintly. "I know that too: all of it."

" 'All?' There's more?"

"Indeed. You've left out the middle. It goes:

> Set a course from the old Dog Star
> A point to the north of Achernar;
> Fare until, on the starboard beam,
> Six red suns toward a blue sun stream.
> Sleight your ship to where afar
> A cluster hangs like a scimitar.
> Under the hilt to the verge extreme
> And dead ahead shines Thamber's gleam.

"Well, well," said Gersen. He rose to his feet, jumped up to the control deck, set dials, threw power back into the Jarnell System.

"Where are we going?" asked Alusz Iphigenia.

"Sirius—the Dog Star."

"You take the rhyme seriously?"

"I've heard no other directions; I've got to take it seriously or do nothing whatever."

"Hmm." Alusz Iphigenia sipped the wine. "In that case, since I've told you all I know, you will put me down at Sirius or perhaps Earth?"

"No."

"But—I know no more than I've told you!"

"You know the look of Thamber's constellations. Your rhyme, if it ever gave accurate directions, is a thousand years old or more. Sirius and Achernar have both shifted. We might arrive somewhere near Thamber—hopefully within ten or twenty light years. Then we'd have to use the old trick of lost star-travelers: they scan the sky until in some quarter they find a familiar constellation. There will only be one, and this in miniature, for it will be directly behind their home planet. All other constellations will be distorted; and even this constellation will have intervening stars superimposed upon it: notably the home sun. Nevertheless—there is always the one familiar constellation to search for, and if you find it, you head for it, and presently, when it grows to its familiar size, your home world is close at hand."

"What if you can't find a familiar constellation?"

"You can still find your way home. You must fly up or down, normal to the plane of the galaxy, until you can see the whole spread of it, and then there are landmarks to be found. This requires much time, much energy, much wear and strain upon the Jarnell. If anything goes wrong—then you are lost indeed, for there is nothing more to do and you float in space looking down on the home galaxy spreading below like a carpet until your energy fails and then you die." Gersen shrugged. "I have never been lost." He raised his glass of wine, eyed it warily, then went to the galley and brought out a new bottle. "Tell me of Thamber."

Alusz Iphigenia spoke for two hours while Gersen leaned back on the settee sipping wine. It was a pleasant experience, watching and listening; for a period the realities of his existence were far away. . . . Alusz Iphigenia mentioned Aglabat, the city behind a wall of dark brown stone, and Gersen roused himself. Enervation was a danger. His stay at Interchange had done him no good. He had become pliable, easily distracted. . . . Nevertheless he relaxed again, sipping wine, listening to Alusz Iphigenia. . . .

Thamber was a wonderful world. No one knew when the first man had arrived; the time was lost in the past. There were various continents, subcontinents, peninsulas, and a great archipelago of tropical islands. Alusz Iphigenia was native to Draszane in Gentilly, a principality on the western shore of the smallest continent. To the east was Vadrus, ruled by Sion Trumble, and beyond the Land of Misk. The remain-

der of the continent, except for a number of feuding states on
the east coast, was wilderness inhabited by barbarians. Similar conditions prevailed on the other continents. Alusz
Iphigenia mentioned a score of peoples, each of distinctive
character. Certain of these produced great music and pag-
eants of heart-stopping grandeur; others were fetishists and
murderers ruled by ogres. In the mountains lived bandit
chieftains and arrogant lordlings, each secure in his castle.
Everywhere were wizards and warlocks, capable of the most
astounding feats, and one weird area to the north of the
largest continent was ruled by fiends and demons. The native
flora and fauna were complex, rich and beautiful, and sometimes dangerous; there were sea-monsters, scaled wolves of
the tundra, the horrid dnazd of the mountains to the north of
Misk.

Technology and the ways of modern living were unknown
on Thamber. Even the Brown Bersaglers of Kokor Hekkus
carried only voulgues and daggers, while the knights of Misk
were armed with swords and crossbows. Between Misk and
Vadrus there was intermittent strife, with Gentilly usually al-
lied with Vadrus. Sion Trumble was a man of heroic valor,
but he never had been able to overcome the Brown Bersaglers. In a tremendous battle, he had repelled the barbarians of the Skar Sakau, who had thereupon turned their full
fury to the south, upon the Land of Misk, where they had
been raiding villages, destroying outposts, and spreading dev-
astation.

Gersen listened with wonder. The romantic legends regarding Thamber had not been exaggerated; if anything they
were understated. He said as much to Alusz Iphigenia, who
shrugged. "Thamber is a world of romantic deeds, certainly.
The castles have great halls where the bards sing and
pavilions where maidens dance to the music of lutes, but below are dungeons and torture chambers. The knights are a
magnificent sight in their armor and their flags, and then in
the snows of Skava Steppe their legs are hacked off by the
Skodolak nomads, and they lie helpless until the wolves tear
them to pieces. The witches brew philters and the wizards
send up the smoke of dreams, and also infect their enemies
with blights. . . . Two hundred years ago the great heroes
lived. Tyler Trumble conquered Vadrus and built the city
Carrai where Sion Trumble now rules. Jadask Dousko found
Misk a land of herdsmen and Aglabat a fishiing village. In ten
years he had created the first Brown Corps, and there has

been war ever since." She sighed. "In Draszane life is relatively calm; we have four ancient colleges, hundreds of *bibliothèques*. Gentilly is a peaceful old country, but Misk and Vadrus somehow are different. Sion Trumble wants me for his queen—but would there ever be peace and happiness? Or would he always be fighting Skodolaks or the Tadousko Oi or the Sea-Helms? And always Kokor Hekkus, who now will be implacable. . . ."

Gersen was silent.

Alusz Iphigenia went on. "At Interchange I read books—of Earth and the Concourse and Aloysius. I know how you live. And at first I wondered why Kokor Hekkus stayed so long at Aglabat, why he fought with swords when he could fit out the Brown Bersaglers with energy weapons. But there is no mystery. He needs emotion as other men need food. He craves excitement and horror and hate and lust. He finds it in the Land of Misk. But someday he will dare too much and Sion Trumble will kill him." She laughed sadly. "Or someday Sion Trumble will attempt a particularly ludicrous act of valor and Kokor Hekkus will kill him—which will be a pity."

"Hmmf," said Gersen. "You are fond of this Sion Trumble?"

"Yes. He is kind and generous and brave. He would not think to rob even Interchange."

Gersen grinned sourly. "I'm more the Kokor Hekkus type. . . . What of the rest of the planet?"

"Everywhere it is different. In Birzul, the Godmus keeps a harem of ten thousand concubines. Every day he enlists ten maidens and discharges ten, or if he happens to be in a bad humor drowns them. In Calastang, the Divine Eye rides through the city carried on a vermilion altar forty yards long and forty yards high. The Lathcar Gentry keep racing-men—slave runners especially bred and trained for the Lath Race Meets. The Tadousko-Oi build their villages on the highest crags and steepest cliffs, and throw down the crippled and infirm. They are Thamber's fiercest warriors, the Tadousko-Oi, and they have leagued themselves to raze the walls of Aglabat. And they will succeed, because the Brown Bersaglers cannot withstand them."

"Have you ever seen Kokor Hekkus close at hand?"

"Yes."

"What does he look like?"

"Give me paper and pen; I will show you."

Gersen brought her writing materials. She made tentative

marks, then worked more swiftly. Line joined line, areas became defined: a face looked forth from the paper. It was an intelligent alert face; under a tall square forehead the eyes were wide and inquiring. The hair was rich, dark, lustrous; the nose was short and straight, the mouth rather small. Alusz Iphigenia sketched in the torso, the legs, to depict a man somewhat over average height, with broad shoulders, a narrow waist, long legs. The body might well have been that of both Billy Windle and Seuman Otwal; the face in no way resembled the keen jutting countenance of Seuman Otwal, and Gersen had never distinctly seen Billy Windle.

Alusz Iphigenia watched him as he studied the picture, and gave a shudder. "I can't understand cruelty—killing—hate. You are almost as frightening as Kokor Hekkus."

Gersen put the sketch aside. "When I was small, my home was destroyed, and all my kin—except for my grandfather. Even then I knew the course of my life was arranged. I knew that I would one by one kill the five men who had conducted the raid. This has been my life, I have no other. I am not evil; I am beyond good and evil—like the killing machine Kokor Hekkus built."

"And I am unlucky enough to be useful to you," said Alusz Iphigenia.

Gersen grinned. "You probably will prefer being useful to me than to Kokor Hekkus, since all I ask is that you guide me to Thamber."

"You are gallant," said Alusz Iphigenia, and Gersen could not decide whether her remark carried a barb or not.

Sirius burnt white ahead, with off to the side the yellow-white star that had nurtured the human race. Alusz Iphigenia contemplated it wistfully, turned to Gersen as if to plead with him, then thought better of it and held her tongue.

Gersen pointed to Achernar, at the source of the River Eridanus. "A point $11\frac{1}{4}°$ north is the plane of galactic north containing the Sirius-Achernar line. But the rhyme must be a thousand years old, perhaps longer—so first we take ourselves to the position of Sirius a thousand years ago. Not too difficult. Then we calculate Achernar's apparent position of a thousand years ago—again not too difficult. Using these two new points, then we angle north $11\frac{1}{4}°$ and hope for the best. And since I've already made the computations. . . ." He carefully adjusted the verniers; Sirius swung grandly away to the side.

Presently the Jarnell snapped out; the Starskip drifted in unfractured ether. Gersen turned the bow toward the point Achernar had occupied a thousand years before; then swung up 11¼° in a plane parallel to the north-south galactic axis. "Here goes." He engaged the intersplit; the Starskip and its contents, deprived of inertia and Einsteinian constrictions, slid with near-instantaneity along the generated fracture. "Now we must watch for six red stars. They may or may not be streaming toward a blue star; they may or may not be on the starboard beam, unless the rhyme intends that the dorsal-ventral plane of the ship lie parallel to the north-south galactic axis. . . ."

Time went by. Near stars slid across stars more distant, which in turn slid across the even farther specks of light behind.

Gersen became edgy. He expressed doubt that Alusz Iphigenia had remembered the rhyme correctly. She replied with a shrug indicating small concern one way or the other, and presently offered the conjecture that Gersen had made a mistake in his computations.

"How long was your trip to Interchange?" He had asked her this before, but always she had given him a vague answer, as now she did again. "I slept a great deal. Time seemed to go swiftly."

Gersen began to suspect that the rhyme had taken them on a wild goose chase, that Thamber lay in a different quarter of the galaxy, and that Alusz Iphigenia knew this fact very well.

Alusz Iphigenia was aware of his dubiousness, and it was with a note of vindication that she pointed ahead to six beautiful red giants strung out in a down-curving line toward a great blue star.

Gersen's only comment was a grudging, "Well, they seem to be on our starboard beam, so rhyme and calculations both aren't too far off." He disengaged the Jarnell; the Starskip drifted. "Now: a cluster shaped like a scimitar: probably a naked-eye object."

"There." Alusz Iphigenia pointed. "Thamber is nearby."

"How do you know?"

"The cluster like the scimitar. In Gentilly we call it the God-Boat. Though from here it looks different."

Gersen turned the ship toward the "hilt"; once again he cut in the intersplit; the boat slipped forward. Directly through the cluster they flew, with stars all around, and then came out into a region only sparsely populated. "It's a fact," said Gersen. "We're at the edge of the galaxy: the 'verge extreme.' Somewhere, dead ahead, should be 'Thamber's gleam.'"

Dead ahead lay a sparse scatter of stars.

"The sun is G8—orange," said Gersen. "Which is the orange sun? . . . There. That one."

The orange star appeared something to the side and below. Gersen cut off the intersplit. He adjusted the macroscope, which revealed a single planet. He raised the magnification: continents and seas swam into focus. "Thamber," said Alusz Iphigenia Eperje-Tokay.

CHAPTER 10

There is a human quality that cannot be precisely named: possibly the most noble of all human qualities. It includes but is larger than candor, generosity, comprehension, niceness of distinction, intensity, steadiness of purpose, total commitment. It is participation in all human perceptions, recollection of all human history. It is characteristic of every great creative genius and can never be learned: learning in this regard is bathos—the dissection of a butterfly, a spectroscope turned to the sunset, the psychoanalysis of a laughing girl. The attempt to learn is self-destructive; when erudition comes in, poetry departs. How common the man of intellect who cannot feel! How trifling are his judgments against those of the peasant who derives his strength, like Antaeus, from the emotional sediment of the race! Essentially the tastes and preferences of the intellectual elite, derived from learning, are false, doctrinaire, artificial, shrill, shallow, uncertain, eclectic jejune, and insincere.

... *Life*, Volume IV, by Unspiek, Baron Bodissey

The critics discuss Baron Bodissey's *Life:*

A monumental work if you like monuments. ... One is irresistibly put in mind of the Laocoön group, with the good baron contorted against the coils of common sense, and the more earnest of his readers likewise endeavoring to disengage themselves.
... *Pancretic Review*, St. Stephen, Boniface

Ponderously the great machine ingests its bales of lore; grinding, groaning, shuddering, it brings forth its product: small puffs of acrid vari-colored vapor.
... *Excalibur*, Patris, Krokinole

Six volumes of rhodomontade and piffle.
... *Academia*, London, Earth

Egregious, ranting, boorish, unacceptable—
                    ... *The Rigellian*, Avente, Alphanor

Sneers jealously at the careers of better men. ....
Impossible not to feel honest anger.
                    ... *Galactic Quarterly*, Baltimore, Earth

Tempting to picture Baron Bodissey at work in the
Arcadian habitat he promulgates, surrounded by admir-
ing goat-herds.
                    ... *El Orchide*, Serle, Quantique

It was morning over the continent Despaz. Alusz Iphigenia
pointed out the geographical divisions. "To the south, the
long strip under the Skar Sakau Mountains, along the
seacoast—that is the Land of Misk. Aglabat is hard to see; it
is brown and merges with the landscape, but it is there, where
the coast curves inland." She pointed.

"And where is your home?"

"To the west. First is Vadrus over that arm of mountains.
You can see the city Carrai: a patch of white and gray. Then
there are more mountains and Gentilly lies beyond. There,
where the sunlight is just touching—Gentilly." She turned
away from the macroscope. "But naturally you will never go
there. Nor to Carrai."

"Why not?"

"Because neither my father nor Sion Trumble would allow
me to be your slave."

Without comment, Gersen bent over the macroscope,
studied the landscape for the better part of an hour, while the
planet rolled over into the sunlight.

"A number of things are clear," he said at last, "and a
number of things aren't so clear. For instance, how I can approach Kokor Hekkus without being killed? He undoubtedly
has radar and quite possibly sky-bolts to protect his city. We
must land somewhere beyond the range of detection devices,
and the most convenient spot seems to be beyond those
mountains."

"And after you land—what then?"

"In order to kill Kokor Hekkus, first I find him. To find
him, I'll have to look for him."

"What of me?" complained Alusz Iphigenia woefully. "I
left Thamber to escape Kokor Hekkus; now you bring me
back. After you are killed, which is certain, what then? Must
I return to Interchange?"

"It seems that our interests coincide," said Gersen. "We both want Kokor Hekkus dead. Neither wants him aware of our presence on Thamber. We will stay together."

He turned the Starskip down toward Thamber, standing well to the north of the mountains called the Skar Sakau. After careful inspection of the terrain, he found an isolated col under a great peak and there he landed. To right and left stood other wind-lashed peaks, laced with glaciers; below and to the south spread a jumble of ridges, chasms, precipices: as wild a region as any Gersen had known. While waiting for air pressure to equalize, he lowered the little air-car from its pod, armed himself with his various weapons, wrapped himself in a cape, as did Alusz Iphigenia. He opened the port, jumped down upon the soil of Thamber. The sun was bright; the air was cold; the wind mercifully was still. Alusz Iphigenia joined him, to stand looking around with an air of repressed exhilaration, as if in spite of her fears she was happy to be home. She turned to Gersen and spoke impulsively. "You're not an evil man, in spite of what you say about yourself. You've treated me kindly—more kindly than I could have expected. Why not give over this fantastic scheme of yours? Kokor Hekkus is secure behind the walls of Aglabat, not even Sion Trumble can threaten him. What can you do? To kill him you must bring him forth, you must defeat all his cruel ruses. And never forget that in all the universe he most wishes to meet you."

"I'm aware of this," said Gersen.

"And you still persist? You must be a lunatic or a sorcerer."

"No."

"Then you have made plans?"

"How can I make plans when I have no facts? That's what we're going out for now. See this box?" He nudged a black metal case with his toe. "I can sit at a distance of ten miles and send a spy-cell into Aglabat, to learn whatever I need to know."

Alusz Iphigenia had no rebuttal to make. Gersen appraised the Starskip, the surrounding mountains; surely no wandering barbarians would come so high or so far. Divining his thoughts, Alusz Iphigenia said, "They keep to the south of the Skar, where their flocks find sustenance, where the granaries of Misk are near at hand. If we fly south, we will see their villages. They are the most ferocious fighters alive, using only daggers and bare hands."

Gersen packed the black case aboard the air-boat, which, unlike the flying platform carried by his old Model 9B, was equipped with a transparent dome and comfortable seats. Alusz Iphigenia stepped aboard, Gersen joined her, closed down the dome. The boat rose, skidded off down the col, then south through the soaring juts and crags. Never had Gersen seen such awesome scenery. Cliffs rose sheer from crevasse-like valley in which wound a dim metal tendril of a river, visible only because the orange sun hung at noon. Chasm opened into chasm; winds roaring through collided and buffeted the air-car. Occasionally a waterfall plunged from the lip of a crag, to fray and wave like a wisp of white silk.

Crag after crag, ridge after ridge slipped behind, and the lay of the valleys was to the south. Far below, forests and meadows could be seen, and presently Alusz Iphigenia pointed to what seemed a complicated crumble of rock pasted to an almost sheer crag. "A village of the Tadousko-Oi. They'll think us a magic bird."

"So long as they don't shoot us down."

"They use only boulders to roll upon their enemies and bows and catapults for their hunting." Gersen nevertheless gave the village a wide berth, swinging across toward the opposite cliff wall, the surface of which seemed curiously humped and pocked. Only when within a hundred yards did he realize he was approaching another village, clinging with credible precariousness to the barren rock. He glimpsed a few dark figures; on a roof a man aimed a weapon. Gersen cursed, swerved; but a short sharp metal dart spat through the fore-part of the air-boat, which gave a jerk, a lurch, then sagged.

Alusz Iphigenia cried out, Gersen hissed between his teeth. Not two hours on Thamber and already faced with disaster! "The front lift-vanes are gone," he said, trying to speak calmly. "We're in no danger, don't be frightened. We'll return to the ship."

But this was obviously impossible: the air-boat hung at an alarming angle, suspended on the center and rear vanes alone.

"We'll have to land," said Gersen. "I may be able to repair the damage. . . . I thought you said these people had no weapons."

"It must have been a cross-bow captured from Kokor

Hekkus. I can think of no other explanation. . . . I'm truly sorry."

"It's no fault of yours." Gersen gave his full attention to the plunging air-boat, trying to hold it on a manageable slant as they settled into the valley. At the last instant, he cut off the rear jets, pushed the propulsion hard over, and for an instant held the craft on an even keel, and so they came down easily on a gravel terrace fifty feet above the river.

Gersen stiffly alighted, went to inspect the damage. His heart sank.

"How bad is it?" asked Alusz Iphigenia anxiously.

"Very bad. I might be able to get us back to the ship, by sliding the center vane forward, or something similar. . . . Well to work." He brought out such tools as the standard equipment afforded, and set to work. An hour passed. Noon sunlight left the valley, blue shadows collected; with them came a dank chill smelling of snow and wet stone. Alusz Iphigenia tugged at Gersen's arm. "Quick! Hide! The Tadousko-Oi."

Startled, Gersen let himself be dragged into a cleft among the rocks. A moment later he saw one of the strangest sights of his lifetime. Down the valley came twenty or thirty large centipedes, each mounted by five men. The centipedes, Gersen noted, were similar to the fort built by Patch Construction, but much smaller. They ran smoothly over the stones, almost flowing. The riders were an ill-favored lot—massively muscled men whose maroon skins were burnished like old leather. Their eyes were stony and staring, their mouths harsh, their noses heavy and hooked. They wore clumsy garments of black leather, helmets of crude iron and black leather; each carried a lance, an ax, and a heavy dagger.

At the sight of the disabled air-car, the band drew up in surprise. "At least they weren't sent out to pick us up," whispered Gersen.

Alusz Iphigenia said nothing. They were pressed close together in the cleft: even in the extremity of the circumstances he felt a tingling at the contact.

The Tadousko-Oi had surrounded the air-car. A number alighted, and conversed in a harsh mumble. They began to look up and down the valley. It was only a matter of seconds before one of them would investigate the cleft.

Gersen whispered to Alusz Iphigenia, "Stay here. I'll distract them." He stepped forward, stood with thumbs hooked in his weapon harness. For a moment the warriors stood staring, then one who wore a helmet more complicated than the others came slowly forward. He spoke: harsh grumbling words apparently derived from the ancient universal tongue, but incomprehensible to Gersen. The slate-colored eyes of the chief—this seemed to be his rank—flicked past Gersen in new surprise. Alusz Iphigenia had come forward. She spoke in a rough approximation of the Tadousko-Oi language; the chief replied. The remaining warriors sat motionless; Gersen had never seen a tableau more sinister.

Alusz Iphigenia spoke to Gersen. "I have told him that we are enemies of Kokor Hekkus, that we come from a far world to kill him. The hetman says that they are embarked on a raid, that they are to join with other bands, and that they plan to attack Aglabat."

Gersen appraised the hetman once more. "Ask him if he can provide transportation back to our ship. I'll pay him well."

Alusz Iphigenia spoke; the hetman gave a grunt of grim humor. He spoke; Alusz Iphigenia translated.

"He refuses. All the company are intent on this great raid. He says that if we like we can join the raiding party. I told him that you preferred to repair the air-boat."

The hetman spoke: Gersen caught the word 'dnazd' used several times. Alusz Iphigenia turned—after a curious hesitation—to Gersen. "He says that we can't survive the night here, that the dnazd will kill us."

"What is the 'dnazd'?"

"A great beast. This place is called the Valley of the Dnazd."

The hetman spoke again in his dull grumbling voice; Gersen's ear, accustomed to extracting meaning from the thousand and one dialects and variants of the universal tongue, began to penetrate the hoarseness and glottal overtones. The hetman, for all the ominous sound to his voice, did not seem hostile. Gersen gathered that it was below the dignity of a war party such as this to prev upon helpless wanderers. "You say you are enemies of Kokor Hekkus," seemed to be the essence of his words. "In that case the man will be anxious to join the war party—if, that is to say, he is a fighting man, as he may be in spite of his unhealthv pallor."

Alusz Iphigenia translated. "He savs that this is a w?r party. Your pale skin gives him the impression that you are sick. He says that if we wish to come, it will be in a menial capacity. There will be much work and much danger."

"Hmm. Is that what he says?"

"Words to that effect."

It was apparent that Alusz Iphigenia had no wish to join the war party. Gersen said, "Ask the hetman if there is any means by which we can return to the ship."

Alusz Iphigenia asked the question; the hetman seemed sardonically amused. "If you can escape the dnazd, if you can find your way over two hundred miles of mountains without food and shelter."

Alusz Iphigenia translated in a hollow voice. "He says he can't help us: we can try if we like." She looked at the air-boat. "Can we repair this?"

"I don't think so. Not unless I find tools. We had better go with these people—at least until something better offers."

Alusz Iphigenia reluctantly translated Gersen's words. The chieftain gave an uninterested assent; he motioned, one of the mounts that carried only four warriors approached, Gersen climbed up on the pad that served as saddle, pulled Alusz Iphigenia up into his lap. This was the closest contact he had ever made with her; it seemed amazing that he had restrained himself so long. She seemed to be thinking similar thoughts, and gave him a pensive look. For a space she held herself as rigid as possible, then gradually relaxed.

The centipedes ran smooth as oil: down the valley moved the war party along an almost invisible trail that led up and down, over boulders, through gaps, cracks, and crevices. Occasionally when the valley walls closed tight together, with the Thamber sky a strip of dark blue ribbon and the water a rushing black syrup, the procession ascended the cliffs. The warriors kept utter silence; the centipede-mounts made no sound; there was nothing to be heard but sigh of wind and sound of water. Gersen became ever more conscious of the warm body leaning against him. He reminded himself wistfully that indulgences of this sort were not for him, that his life was predestined to grief and doom—but his cells and nerves and instincts protested, and his arms tightened around Alusz Iphigenia. She looked around; he saw that her face was abstracted, melancholy, that her eyes were bright with something like tears. Why in the world is she melancholy? Gersen wondered. The circumstances were unfortunate, vexatious, but still short of desperate; if anything the Tadousko-Oi had treated them with courtesy. . . . A halt interrupted his thoughts. The hetman was consulting a group of lieutenants; their attention was fixed high above, upon a crag where Gersen made out another of the dull crumbles he now knew for a village.

Alusz Iphigenia shifted in his arms. "This is an enemy village," she told him. "The Tadousko-Oi feud among themselves."

The hetman gave a signal: three scouts dismounted, ran ahead, testing the path. A hundred yards ahead, they croaked out in guttural alarm, sprang back, as a slab of rock crashed across the trail.

The warriors stirred no muscle. The scouts continued along the trail, disappeared. Half an hour later they returned.

The hetman signaled. One after another the mounts surged forward. From far above, objects like gray peas appeared, falling with odd slowness, almost floating. But size and speed were illusory; the objects were boulders that smashed to splinters along the trail. The warriors, showing no concern, avoided the fall by speeding, slowing, darting ahead, halting. When Gersen and Alusz Iphigenia were carried past, the fall of boulders had halted.

Beyond the village the valley broadened to a crescent-shaped meadow with a feathery forest along the river. Here, the lead mount stopped short, and for the first time a grumble of words passed down the line: "Dnazd."

But the dnazd was not in evidence. The party, crouching low on their mounts, timorously continued across the meadow.

The day had gone dark. High above, a few wisps of cirrus burned bronze in the dying sunlight. The party presently entered a cleft in the rocks—hardly more than a crevice—along which the mounts could squeeze only by folding their legs back. At times Gersen might have touched the walls to either side. The crack widened, became a circular area floored with sand. All alighted; the mounts were taken to the side, shackled together. Certain warriors dipped leather buckets in a nearby pool, fed the mounts buckets of water and what looked to be powdered blood. Others made small fires, hung pots on tripods, and began to boil up a rank-smelling stew.

The hetman and his lieutenants sat together, conferring in undertones. The hetman glanced toward Gersen and Alusz Iphigenia, made a movement; two of the warriors set up a kind of tent of black cloth. Alusz Iphigenia exhaled a soft sigh, turned her eyes to the ground.

The stew was cooked; each warrior took an iron bowl from inside his helmet, dipped it into the pot, careless to steam and boiling stew. Having no bowls, Gersen and Alusz Iphigenia sat patiently, while the warriors ate with fingers and slabs of hard bread. The first to finish polished his bowl with sand, brought it politely to Gersen, who accepted with thanks, dipped into the stew, brought the bowl to Alusz Iphigenia, an act which evoked an amused rumble of comment. Another bowl was forthcoming and now Gersen ate. The stew was not unpleasant, though salty and seasoned with an odd peppery spice; the bread was hard, and tasted like burning weeds. The warriors squatted around the fires without laughing or horseplay.

The hetman rose, went to the tent. Gersen looked about for a place for himself and Alusz Iphigenia. It would be a chilly night, for they had only their cloaks. The Tadousko-Oi who had even less evidently planned to lay themselves down before the fire. . . . The warriors were looking at Alusz Iphigenia in a puzzled manner. Gersen looked at her also. She sat staring into the fire, arms wrapped around knees: nothing to excite perplexity. In the opening to the tent the hetman appeared, frowning impatiently. He beckoned to Alusz Iphigenia.

Gersen slowly rose to his feet. Alusz Iphigenia without lifting her eyes from the fire said in a soft voice: "To the Tadousko-Oi, women are a lower species. . . . They keep their women in common, and the highest ranking warrior sleeps with what is available—first."

Gersen looked toward the hetman. "Explain that this is not our custom."

Alusz Iphigenia looked slowly up at him. "We can do nothing; we are—"

"Tell him."

Alusz Iphigenia turned to the hetman, spoke Gersen's words. The warriors sitting around the fire became still. The hetman seemed startled, and came two paces forward. He spoke: "In your own land, you are obliged to observe your own customs; but this is the Skar Sakau, and here our ways must hold. Is this pale man the highest ranking warrior present? No, of course not. Therefore, you, the pale woman must come to my tent. This is the way of the Skar Sakau."

Gersen did not wait for the translation. "Tell him that I am an extremely high-ranked warrior in my own land; that if you sleep with anyone it shall be with me."

To this the hetman responded, not discourteously. "Again, this is the Skar Sakau. I am the hetman, no man can resist me; it is beyond dispute that I out-rank the pale man. So come, woman, let there be an end to this undignified parley."

Gersen said, "Tell him that I am more highly ranked—that I am a Space-Admiral, a Ruler, a Lord—anything that he will understand."

She shook her head, rose to her feet. "I had best obey."

"Tell him."

"You will be killed," said Alusz Iphigenia.

"Tell him."

Alusz Iphigenia spoke. The chieftain came another two steps forward, pointed to a burly young warrior. "Out-rank this man, trounce him thoroughly to emphasize his lowly condition."

The warrior doffed his upper harness. The hetman spoke, "The pale man carries coward's weapons. Let him know that he must fight as a man, either with dagger or his hands. He must remove his fire-flashers."

Gersen's hand trembled toward his projac. But warriors nearby would instantly have overpowered him. Slowly he handed his weapons to Alusz Iphigenia, removed his jacket and singlet. His opponent carried a heavy double-edged dagger; Gersen thereupon brought forth his own slim-bladed weapon.

An area of sand between three fires was cleared; warriors of the Tadousko-Oi squatted about in a circle, liver-colored faces grave, dispassionate, almost insect-like.

Gersen stepped forward, assessed his opponent. He was taller than himself, with hard muscles and quick motions. He twitched the heavy dagger as if it were a feather. Gersen held his blade loosely. The young warrior moved his dagger in a hypnotic circle, steel glimmering in the firelight.

Gersen made a sudden hard motion. His blade flashed through the air, cut through the warrior's wrist, pinned it to his shoulder. The dagger fell from limp fingers; he stared in numb wonder at his helpless hand. Gersen stepped close, picked up the dropped weapon, ducked a kick, struck the warrior over the ear with the flat of the blade. The warrior tottered; Gersen struck him again; the man fell to the ground in a daze.

Gersen recovered his dagger, politely placed the young warrior's weapon into its scabbard, returned to Alusz

Iphigenia, and began to dress himself in the clothes he had removed.

For the first time there was a murmur among the spectators: neither applause, nor disapproval: merely a mild wonder, with a hint of dissatisfaction.

All looked at the hetman, who now marched forward. He spoke in a loud voice, in a careful sing-song rhythm: "Pale man, you have defeated this young warrior. I cannot fault the unconventional method employed, though we of the Tadousko-Oi hold it the way of a weakling to stake all on a single cast. Moreover, nothing has been proved, other than the fact that you outrank the young warrior. You must fight again." He searched among the faces, but Gersen spoke. "Tell the hetman," he instructed Alusz Iphigenia, "that my differences, in connection to where you shall spend the night, are solely with him, and it is he with whom I choose to fight."

Alusz Iphigenia repeated the message in a low voice, and now the audience sat stunned. The hetman was obviously surprised. "Does he so choose? Does he not realize I am champion, the master of all men I have so far faced? Explain to him that I am hetman, that since he is not of the clan, such a fight must be to the death."

Alusz Iphigenia explained; Gersen said, "Inform the hetman that I have no wish to prove my high rank; that I much prefer sleeping to fighting, so long as he does not insist on your company."

Alusz Iphigenia spoke; the hetman removed his shirt. Then he spoke. "We shall settle the question of rank quickly, for there may not be two leaders to a war party. To avoid a coward's cast, we will fight with bare hands."

Gersen appraised him: tall he stood, heavy but agile, with dark flesh that seemed as hard as horn. He glanced down at Alusz Iphigenia who looked up at him fascinated, then slowly he stepped forward. Beside the knotted dark body his own seemed pallid and elastic. To test the hetman Gersen aimed an apparently random blow toward his head; instantly a hard hand seized his wrist, a foot lashed out. Gersen disengaged his wrist with a jerk; he could have seized the foot and flung the hetman over, but instead allowed the toe barely to graze his hip. And he swung another left-handed blow that landed, almost as if by accident, on the hetman's neck. It felt like a tree trunk.

The hetman hopped forward, both feet at a time, in a

peculiarly disconcerting manner, both arms wide. Gersen punched at the out-thrust face. He struck the left eye, but was caught up in an arm lock, of a sort he had never experienced before, which in seconds would snap his ulna. Gersen relaxed his knees, then sprang around in a kind of mad somersault, kicking the hetman in the face and wrenching his arm free. The hetman was less confident when Gersen faced him next. He slowly raised both arms; Gersen struck at the left eye. Again the hetman's foot lashed out, Gersen refrained from seizing the ankle; again it grazed his hip. The hetman's eye was swollen. As he sprang back after the kick, Gersen took advantage of an instant's respite to scrape a hollow into the sand with his foot. The hetman circled him. Gersen moved away, feinted; his wrist was seized; a great hand hacked at the back of his neck. Gersen dove instantly forward, put his shoulder to the hetman's rock-hard belly; the blow slid off his shoulder. Gersen thrust forward; the hetman pulled up a knee battering Gersen's chest. Gersen caught the knee, shifted his position, caught the ankle, twisted; the hetman was forced to fall to protect his knee; Gersen kicked him in the right eye, jumped away from the sweep of the massive red arm. He stood panting and sobbing, his chest aching; but the hetman's right eye was closing. Gersen bent, carefully enlarged the hollow in the sand. Glaring like a boar the hetman watched him; then, apparently casting caution aside, rushed forward: Gersen moved aside; on occasion he had exercised the same feigned recklessness. He jabbed at the hetman's left eye, but a dazzling fast blow of the hetman's left hand crushed his wrist, causing intense pain and leaving his left hand limp. This was a serious loss, but the hetman's right eye was shut and his left eye was swollen. Ignoring the pain, Gersen flapped his now useless left hand into the red face; again the left hand swung up to hack; but Gersen caught the left wrist in his right hand, kicked behind the left knee, butted into the hetman's neck, and the hetman let himself sag, still perfectly controlled and coordinated. Grunting, hissing between his teeth, Gersen hacked into the momentarily exposed neck; the hetman, purple in the face, slashed out back-handed; Gersen, who now was beginning to lose his agility, caught the blow on his right forearm. It was like the impact of a sledge-hammer; left and right hands both were useless. The two men stood back, both sweating and gasping. Both of the hetman's eyes were almost shut; Gersen strove to conceal the futility of his hands; it would be fatal to display weakness. Summoning his last resources he crouched, began to stalk the hetman; his arms held as if ready to strike. The hetman roared out, made his two-footed jump; Gersen lurched to meet him, drove his right elbow into the black contusion of the hetman's neck. The hetman's arms surrounded Gersen, he began banging the side of his head against Gersen's temple. Gersen sagged low, butted at the hetman's chin, kicked at his knees. Both toppled, the hetman trying to swing Gersen under. Gersen acceded to the impulse, augmented it, landed on top, clenched in the wet maroon arms. He butted at the chin, at the nose; the hetman tried to counter with snapping teeth, heaving and lurching to roll to the top, which Gersen prevented with outspread legs. He butted; the teeth scarred his forehead. He butted at the nose; it broke. He butted again, battered down at the chin, again the teeth lacerated his forehead—but the hetman could take no more. He loosened his grip that he might place a forearm under Gersen's neck, but Gersen had been waiting. He jerked himself free, sat upon the hetman's abdomen, then with his last energy brought his head down against the bridge of the hetman's nose.

The hetman choked, relaxed, dazed by pain, fatigue, the blows to neck and head. Gersen staggered to his feet, arms dangling. He looked down at the great maroon body. Never had he fought so terrible an antagonist. Was the hetman dead? Lesser blows had killed lesser men.

Gersen stumbled to where Alusz Iphigenia sat sobbing. In a slurred voice he said, "Tell the warriors to care for their hetman. He is a great fighter, and the enemy of my enemy."

Alusz Iphigenia spoke. From the onlookers came a dismal rumble. Several warriors went to look down at the unconscious hetman, then glanced toward Gersen. He stood swaying. Fires flickered crazily, faces were a nightmare blur. He gasped for air, and looking high glimpsed a cluster of stars shaped like a scimitar. . . .

Alusz Iphigenia had risen to her feet. "Come," she said, and led him to the tent. None barred their way.

CHAPTER 11

From "Smell Your Best," by Rudi Thumm, article in *Cosmopolis*, January, 1521:

Here is an excerpt from the catalog of AEMISTHES: *Perfumes, Redolences, Essences,* Pamfile, Zaccaré, Quantique. Each category is further amplified in the body of the catalog, with the nature and quality of the constituents exactly, even redolently, defined.

Section I: Odors for Personal Use.

Beguilements:
: For the sorcelment of a strange maiden
: To induce a new gallant
: To anounce a triumph
: To stupefy a noisy child
: To welcome a lover
: To hint at revulsion

At festivals:
: Promenades
: Revels
: Tarantellas

In Solitude:

At gatherings:
: Small societies
: Occasions of dignified circumstance
: While discussing family secrets
: At the god-yell
  —morning
  —evening
  —rogue
  —unpremeditated

et cetera

Section II: Ceremonial

Private occasions:
: For the house
  —various essences
: For the lich-way
: For the ancient tree
: At water tasting
  —morning

Public occasions:
: To lave the feet of the Zatcoon
: To cast upon an imminent battlefield
: To facilitate flight
: To scent the wind

```
        —twilight                    : To welcome good fortune
    : At occasions of grief
    : At occasions of remorse
    : To celebrate a murder


                        et cetera
```

What you should learn from the foregoing is plain: when you visit Zaccaré, don't wear perfume—you may find yourself involved in circumstances you didn't bargain for. The people of this fantastic and beautiful land are as sensitive to odors as the Sirenese are to music, and an apparently insignificant daub of scent affords an astonishing amount of information. As can be seen, every occasion requires its correct perfume, and a mistake will seem utterly ludicrous to the folk of Zaccaré. Unless advised by a local, go scentless. Better neutrality than *gaucherie!*

Perfume manufacture is big business in Zaccaré. At Pamfile, a hundred firms have their headquarters. From all over the Oikumene, oils, extracts, and essences are imported, with as many more collected in the nearby Talalangi Forest.

Here are samples of Zaccaré fragrances:

(scented tabs attached to page of magazine).

Before dawn the warriors stirred, blew the coals ablaze, set their stew a-simmer. The hetman, his head a mass of bruises, sat with his back to a rock, looking dourly across the area. No one spoke to him, nor he to anyone. From the tent came Gersen, followed by Alusz Iphigenia. She had bound his left wrist, massaged his right arm; aside from a thousand bruises, aches, and the sprain of his left wrist, he was not in bad condition. He walked to where the hetman sat, and essayed to speak in the harsh dialect of the Skar Sakau. "You fought well."

"You fought better," mumbled the hetman. "Never since boyhood have I been beaten. I called you a coward. I was wrong. You did not kill me; by this token you become a clan-fellow, and hetman. What are your orders?"

"Suppose I ordered the party to conduct us to our ship?"

"You would not be obeyed. The men would ride off. I was as you are now—war leader. Beyond this I had only such authority as I was willing to enforce. And no more have you."

"In that case," said Gersen, "we will consider the events of last night no more than friendly exercise. You are hetman, we are your guests. When it suits us we shall part company."

The hetman lurched to his feet. "If these are your wishes, so be it. We proceed against our enemy Kokor Hekkus, Ruler of Misk."

The party presently was ready to proceed. A scout went to reconnoiter the valley, but returned hurriedly. "Dnazd!"

"Dnazd!" went the subdued rumble of voices.

An hour passed; the sky brightened. The scout went forth again, returned to signal that all was clear. Out into the winding valley moved the procession, and away.

At noon the valley widened and, as the war party rounded a bend, the notch made by the rocky slopes revealed a far view over a sunny green land.

Ten minutes later they came to a spot where sixty or seventy other centipedes stood tethered with warriors, squatting nearby. The hetman rode forward, conferred with others of similar rank; without delay the entire troop moved off down the valley. An hour before sunset, they came down out of the foothills into a rolling savannah. Here grazed herds of small black ruminants, tended by men and boys riding taller animals of the same general type. At the sight of the Tadousko-Oi they fled incontinently, then finding no pursuit, halted to stare in wonder.

Gradually the land became more populated. First there were a few huts, then round low-walled houses with tall conical roofs, then villages; everywhere there was flight; none dared face the Tadousko-Oi.

At sunset the city Aglabat appeared, rising from a level green plain. Battlemented walls of brown stone surrounded the city, which seemed a compact mass of tall round towers. At the center, from the tallest tower of all, flew a brown and black pennon.

"Kokor Hekkus is in residence," said Alusz Iphigenia. "When he is gone, no pennon flies."

Over green sward as neat and green as the turf of a park, the warriors approached the city.

Alusz Iphigenia was disturbed. "Best that we part company with the Tadousko-Oi before they invest the town."

"Why?" asked Gersen.

"Do you think Kokor Hekkus is to be caught napping? At any minute the Brown Bersaglers will sally forth. There will be a terrible battle, we may well be killed, or worse, captured, without once coming anywhere near Kokor Hekkus."

Gersen could not quarrel with her remarks, but by some peculiar circumstance he had attached himself to the war band. To leave now—especially when he shared the views of Alusz Iphigenia as to the probable destruction of the Tadousko-Oi—seemed like treachery. Still, he had not come to Thamber for chivalric gestures.

With the city two miles distant, the party halted. Gersen approached the hetman, "What are your battle-plans?"

"We besiege the city. Sooner or later Kokor Hekkus must send forth his army. Before, when this occurred, we were too few and were forced to flee. We still are few, but not too few. We will destroy the Brown Bersaglers, we will grind the knights into dust; we will drag Kokor Hekkus across the plain to his death; then we will possess ourselves of the riches of Aglabat."

The plan had the virtue of simplicity, thought Gersen. "Suppose the army does not come forth?"

"Sooner or later it must, unless they prefer to starve."

The sun went down into a purple sky; lights shone from the towers of Aglabat. Tonight no one offered discourtesy to Alusz Iphigenia, like the night before they occupied the black tent.

The sense of her nearness finally destroyed Gersen's self-control; he took her by the shoulders, looked into the dimness of her face, kissed her, and she seemed to respond. But did she? Her expression could not be seen through the dark. He kissed her again, and felt moisture on her face: she was weeping. Angrily he stood back. "Why are you crying?"

"Pent-up emotions, probably."

"Because I kissed you?"

"Of course."

Suddenly everything was unsatisfactory. She was in his power, subject to his orders. He did not want her submission; he wanted her ardor. "Suppose circumstances were different," he said. "Suppose we were in Draszane. suppose that you had no worries. Suppose I came to you—like this—and kissed you. What would you do?"

"I will never see Draszane again," she said sullenly. "I have many worries. I am your slave. Do as you like."

Gersen sat down on the floor of the tent. "Very well. I will go to sleep."

The following day the Tadousko-Oi moved closer to the

city, camping a mile in front of its main gate. On the walls, soldiers could be seen moving back and forth. At noon the gates opened; out marched six regiments of pike-men wearing brown uniforms with black armor and black helmets. The Tadousko-Oi gave a hoarse whoop, sprang to their mounts. Gersen and Alusz Iphigenia watched the battle from the camp. It was savage and bloody, waged without quarter. The Bersaglers fought bravely but without the wild ferocity of the mountain men; presently the remnants retreated through the gates, leaving a field strewn with dead.

The following day was eventless. The brown and black pennon flew from the spire of the citadel. Gersen asked Alusz Iphigenia, "Where does Kokor Hekkus keep his spaceship?"

"On an island to the south. He has an air-car like yours to fly back and forth. Until Sion Trumble attacked the island and captured the spaceship I thought Kokor Hekkus a great wizard."

Gersen was more dissatisfied than ever. It was clear that under no circumstances could he make contact with Kokor Hekkus. Should the Tadousko-Oi succeed in storming the city, Kokor Hekkus would escape in his air-car. . . . It was essential that they return to the Starship. Then he would take up a position where he could see but not be seen, where he could intercept the air-car that must eventually leave Aglabat, no matter what the outcome of the battle.

He told Alusz Iphigenia of his decision; she approved. "We need only fare to Carrai. Sion Trumble will escort you north of the Skar Sakau, and matters will be as you wish."

"What of you?"

She looked away toward the north. "Sion Trumble has long desired me for his bride. He has professed his love. I am willing."

Gersen made a contemptuous sound. Noble Sion Trumble had professed his love! Gallant Sion Trumble! Gersen went to speak to the hetman. "There were casualties in the battle, and I notice that now there are extra mounts. If you could spare me one of these, I will try to return to my spaceship."

"It shall be as you wish. Select the mount of your choice."

"The most docile and easily managed of the group will serve."

Toward evening the mount was brought to the tent; at dawn Gersen and Alusz Iphigenia would depart for Carrai.

During the night workmen from the city stole forth to erect an enclosure a hundred feet on a side, shrouded with brown cloth to a height of twenty feet. The Tadousko-Oi were furious at the insolence. They mounted their centipedes and sallied forth, cautiously however, because the enclosure had not been set out for nothing.

Indeed it had not. When the ranks of the centipede mounts had drawn close the brown cloth bulged: out ran an enormous centipede with thirty-six legs, eyes flashing fire.

The Tadousko-Oi recoiled, swung about in confusion. "Dnazd!" came the cry. "Dnazd!"

"No dnazd," Gersen told Alusz Iphigenia. "That is the product of Patch Engineering and Construction. And it is time we were on our way." They mounted the waiting centipede, sent it scurrying off to the north-west. On the sward before the city the fort ran back and forth, while the Tadousko-Oi scuttled frantically, finally fleeing in complete disorder. In pursuit came the fort, running with a fluid ease that gave Gersen rueful pleasure. Alusz Iphigenia was not yet convinced. "Are you sure the thing is metal?"

"Absolutely."

Certain of the Tadousko-Oi came the way Gersen and Alusz Iphigenia had traveled, and the fort followed, darting bolts of purple-white fire. With every flash, a centipede shriveled and five men died; presently no more were left except that ridden by Gersen and Alusz Iphigenia, a half-mile in advance. They made frantically for the foothills, the fort swerved to cut them off. Up a swell of high ground, Gersen urged the mount, around a knob of rock; here he jumped to the ground, lifted down Alusz Iphigenia. The centipede raced away. Gersen scrambled up to a hiding-place behind an outcrop of moss-covered sandstone, with Alusz Iphigenia crawling after. She looked at him, started to speak; then said nothing. She was dirty and scratched and disheveled; her garments were soiled, her eyes were wide, the pupils dark with fear. Gersen had no time for reassurances. He brought forth his projac, waited.

There came a whir, a thud of thirty-six racing feet; over the rise scrambled the fort, to pause and search the landscape for its prey.

Gersen fleetingly wondered if long ago in Patch's Workshop B he had subconsciously envisioned just this sort of confrontation. He set the projac at low power, took careful aim at a spot along the fort's dorsal ridge, pulled the trigger. In the cut-off cell a relay threw a switch. The legs became limber, the segmented body sagged to the ground. Presently

the hatch opened; members of the crew alighted, to walk
about the fort in obvious puzzlement. Gersen counted them:
nine, out of a crew of eleven. Two had remained inside. All
wore brown coveralls, all carried themselves in an indefinable
manner that was not of Thamber. There were two who might
be Seuman Otwal, or Billy Windle, or Kokor Hekkus: from
distance of fifty yards, Gersen could not be sure of their
faces. One turned: his neck was too long: definitely not the
man Gersen sought. The other? But he had gone back into
the fort. The ionization began to dissipate, the legs were
recovering their strength. . . . "Listen!" Alusz Iphigenia
breathed into Gersen's ear.

Gersen could hear nothing. "Listen!" she said again. Now
Gersen heard a soft click-click click-click—a sound of vast
menace. It seemed to come from behind them. Down the
mountainside came the creature that the fort duplicated: a
true dnazd. Gersen found it hard to understand how anyone
could be deceived by the metal structure. If the Tadousko-Oi
had been fooled by the fort, not so the dnazd. It came scut-
tling forward, stopped short, apparently from curiosity and
amazement. The crew had scrambled aboard and clamped the
hatch. The legs were still limp; from the eye came only a
weak spatter of fire, to strike the dnazd on its rear segment.
It reared high, emitted a wild whistling scream, flung itself on
the fort. Both toppled to the ground, both rolled and
clambered. Mandibles chewed at the metal hull, poison-tipped
prongs stabbed and scratched. Within, the crew tumbled and
rolled until someone managed to set in motion the automatic
righting sequence. Power back to normal, the fort scrambled
to its feet. Once again the dnazd flung itself high to hurtle
down at the metal segments. Fire spat from the eye; the
dnazd lost the use of a leg. Again the eve took aim. A central
segment was blasted, and the dnazd sagged, legs thrashing at
the ground. The fort moved back: fire flared from both sides
of the eyes; the dnazd became a mound of reeking flesh.

Gersen inched forward. Once more he turned his projac on
the cut-off cell. As before, the fort swayed to the ground.
Presently the hatch opened: the crew limped down the ladder
to the ground. Gersen counted: —nine—ten—eleven. All had
come forth. They conferred, then went to inspect the dead
dnazd. When they turned about, Gersen stood nearby, his
projac trained on them.

"Face away from me," said Gersen. "Stand in a line with
hands in the air. I'll kill whoever gives me trouble."

There was indecision; tentative swaying and tensing as each man calculated his chances of becoming a hero. Each decided they were poor. Gersen underscored the fact with a flash of energy that scorched the ground at their feet. Grudgingly, faces contorted into masks of hate, they turned their backs. Alusz Iphigenia came to join Gersen; "Look inside," he said. "Make sure all are out."

She returned after a moment to report the fort empty.

"Now," said Gersen to the eleven men. "You must do exactly as I say, if you value your lives. The first man to the right back up six steps." He was sullenly obeyed. Gersen took his weapon, a small but vicious projac of a design Gersen had never seen before. "Lie down, flat on your face, put your arms to the small of your back."

One by one the eleven moved back, lay flat, were disarmed and bound with straps from their own garments.

One by one Gersen turned the men over so that they lay on their backs; one by one he searched their faces. None were Seuman Otwal.

"Which of you is Kokor Hekkus?" he asked.

There was a pause; then the man who had carried the projac spoke. "He is at Aglabat."

Gersen turned to Alusz Iphigenia. "You know Kokor Hekkus: do any of these men resemble him?"

Alusz Iphigenia looked searchingly at the man who had spoken. "His face is different—but his manner, his way of carrying himself is the same."

Gersen considered the man's features. They appeared genuine, without the subtle demarcations or change of texture that indicated falseness; nor did he wear a mask. But the eyes: were they the eyes of Seuman Otwal? There was an indefinable similarity, a sense of cynical wisdom. Gersen said no more. He looked over the remainder of the crew, then returned to the man who had spoken. "What is your name?"

"Franz Paderbush." The voice was soft, almost obsequious.

"You are native to where?"

"I am Knight Junior of the Castle Pader, at the east of Misk. . . . Do you not believe me?"

"Not with any conviction."

"You need only come to Castle Paderbush," said the captive with a rather unsuitable flippancy of manner, "and the Knight Senior, my father, will vouch for me a dozen times over."

"Possibly true," said Gersen. "Still, you resemble Billy

Windle of Skouse and also a certain Seuman Otwal whom I last met near Krokinole. You others," he said, "get to your feet, start walking."

"Where?" asked one.

"Wherever you choose."

"With our arms bound the savages will kill us," grumbled another.

"Find a ditch and hide till nightfall."

The ten disconsolately departed. Gersen made another search of Paderbush, but found no more weapons. "Now, Knight Junior, to your feet and into the fort."

Paderbush obeyed with a nimble willingness that Gersen found disquieting. He tied the Knight Junior securely to a bench, then clamped the port, and went to the familiar controls.

"You know how to operate this horror?" asked Alusz Iphigenia.

"I helped build it."

She gave him a thoughtful puzzled look, then turned to inspect Franz Paderbush, who favored her with a witless smirk.

Gersen worked the controls; the legs responded, the fort ran off to the north.

"Where are you going?" asked Alusz Iphigenia after a moment.

"To the spaceship, naturally."

"Through the Skar Sakau?"

"Through, or around."

"You must be mad."

Gersen was dampened. "In the fort we should be able to make it."

"You know nothing of the trails. They are difficult and often lead to pitfalls. The Tadousko-Oi will roll down boulders. The chasms are infested by dnazd. If you avoid these, there are crevasses, precipices, crags. We have no food."

"What you say is true. But—"

"Turn west to Carrai. Sion Trumble will honor you, and guide you north around the Skar."

Gersen, unable to refute the arguments, with poor grace swung the fort around, descended into the valley.

They came into a pleasant rolling country. The Skar Sakau dwindled and faded into the blue haze. All through the warm summer afternoon the fort ran west, past small farms and granges, with stone barns and stone cottages with tall roofs, and occasional villages. At the sight of the fort the inhabitants stood glassy-eyed, transfixed with terror. They were an ordinary-seeming folk, fair-skinned with dark hair: the women wearing voluminous skirts and tight patterned bodices; the men, puffed knee-length bloomers, bright shirts, and embroidered jackets. From time to time, a manor house could be seen at the back of a park: occasionally there was a castle perched high on a bluff. Certain of these manors and castles appeared to be falling into ruins. "Ghosts," Alusz Iphigenia explained. "This is ancient country, well haunted!"

Gersen, glancing toward Franz Paderbush, surprised a quiet smile on his face. Several times he had noted a similar smile on the face of Seuman Otwal—but these were neither the features nor the flesh of Seuman Otwal.

The sun sank and twilight fell across the countryside. Gersen halted the fort at the edge of a lonely water-meadow. Rations intended for the crew constituted an evening meal, after which Paderbush was confined to the stern lazaret.

Gersen and Alusz Iphigenia went outside and watched fireflies. Overhead hung the constellations of Thamber: plentiful to the south, sparse to the north where intergalactic space began. A night-creature sang in a nearby forest, the air was soft with the bosky odor of vegetation. Gersen could think of nothing to say. Finally he heaved a sigh, took her hand, which she made no effort to withdraw.

For hours they sat with their backs to the fort. Fireflies flickered across the meadow. From a distant village, a sad-voiced bell tolled the passage of the hours. At last Gersen spread his cloak and they slept in the soft grass.

At dawn they once more set forth to the west. The country changed; the landscape rolled up into forested hills and valleys, then became mountains shrouded with tall conifer-like trees. The habitations became fewer, more primitive; the manor houses disappeared; only the castles remained to brood over valley and river. On one occasion, the silently running fort came upon a band of armed men parading drunkenly down the middle of the road. They wore ragged garments and carried bows and arrows.

"Outlaws," said Alusz Iphigenia. "The Scum of Misk and Vadrus."

A pair of stone keeps guarded the border; the fort ran past; behind, bugles blared hurried calls-to-arms.

An hour later the fort came out upon a view over rolling country to north and west. Alusz Iphigenia pointed: "There is Vadrus. See, behind the dark forest, the patch of white? That is the city Carrai. Gentilly is yet to the west, but I am well known at Carrai. Sion Trumble has often extended hospitality to my family, for in Gentilly I am princess."

"So now you will become his bride."

Alusz Iphigenia looked ahead toward Carrai in regret and sadness, as at some bittersweet recollection. "No. I am no longer a child. All does not seem so easy. Before there was Sion Trumble—and Kokor Hekkus. Sion Trumble is a warrior and no doubt is as brutal in battle as any. But to the folk of Vadrus he makes an attempt at justice. Kokor Hekkus of course is the definition of evil. Before I would have taken Sion Trumble. Now I want neither. I have had too much excitement. . . . Indeed," she said wistfully, "I fear that I have learned too much since leaving Thamber, and I have lost my youth."

Gersen turned. He caught sight of the prisoner. "And why are you amused?"

"I recall a similar disillusionment of my youth," said Franz Paderbush.

"Do you care to relate the circumstances?"

"No. It is only just barely relevant to the conversation."

"How long have you served Kokor Hekkus?"

"All my life. He rules Misk, he is my master."

"Perhaps you can tell us something of his plans?"

"I fear not. I doubt if he has many, and these he keeps to himself. He is a remarkable man. I imagine that he will resent the loss of his fort."

Gersen laughed. "Far less than the other harms I have dealt him. As at Skouse, when I thwarted his bargain with Daeniel Trembath. As at Interchange, when I stole his princess and paid him off with blank paper." As Gersen spoke he studied the eyes of Paderbush; was it his imagination or did the pupils dilate slightly? The uncertainty was exasperating, especially when it seemed so pointless and ungrounded. Billy Windle, Seuman Otwal, Franz Paderbush: none resembled the other save in physical proportion and in a certain indefinable style. None, according to Alusz Iphigenia, could be Kokor Hekkus. . . . The fort slid down from the mountains, passed through a region of orchards and vines, then a well-watered meadowland dotted with crofts and villages; then it came out on a low headland to overlook Carrai—a city far different from Aglabat. Instead of grim brown walls, here were wide avenues, marble colonnades, villas surrounded by trees, palaces in formal gardens as splendid as any of Earth. If there were slums or hovels, they were remote from the main thoroughfares.

At the entrance to the city, a great marble arch supported a ball of rock crystal. Here stood a platoon of guards in purple and green uniforms. At the approach of the fort, a lieutenant bawled orders; the guards marched forward, pallid but determined, seated their pikes, and awaited death.

Fifty yards from the gate, Gersen halted the fort, opened the hatch, leapt to the ground. The soldiers went limp in astonishment. Alusz Iphigenia came forward; the lieutenant seemed to recognize her in spite of her disheveled appearance. "Is it Princess Iphigenia of Draszane, who steps forth from the gullet of the dnazd?"

"The beast belies appearances," said Alusz Iphigenia. "It is Kokor Hekkus' mechanical toy that we have taken from him. Where is Lord Sion Trumble; is he in residence?"

"No, Princess, he is to the north, but his Chancellor only this moment has entered Carrai, and stands nearby. I will send for him."

A tall white-bearded nobleman in black and purple velvet presently appeared. He came gravely forward, made a gesture of respect. Alusz Iphigenia greeted him with relief, as if here at last was someone in whom she could repose confidence. She introduced him to Gersen: "The Baron Endel Thobalt"; then she inquired for Sion Trumble. Baron Thobalt responded in a voice from which irony was not absent: Sion Trumble had sallied forth on a raid against the Grodnedsa: corsairs of the North Promeneous Sea. He was expected back in the not-too-distant future. Meanwhile the princess should regard the city as her own: this would be Sion Trumble's desire.

Alusz Iphigenia turned to Gersen, a new grace and radiance shining from her face. "I cannot repay you for your services to me, nor would I try—after all, I suppose you did not regard them as such. Still I offer you the hospitality that I now command: whatever your desire you need only announce it."

Gersen replied that it had been his pleasure to serve her; any obligation on her part she had more than canceled by guiding him to Thamber. "But I'll still take advantage of your offer. I want Paderbush confined where he'll be absolutely secure until I decide what to do with him."

"We will be lodged at the State Palace; in the crypts are suitable dungeons." She spoke to the lieutenant of the guards, and the unfortunate Paderbush was hustled away.

Returning to the fort, Gersen disconnected various cables and connections, thereby disabling the mechanism. Meanwhile a carriage had appeared, a tall ornate vehicle on golden wheels. Gersen joined Alusz Iphigenia and Baron Thobalt in the forward compartment; with a feeling of guilt for his soiled garments he seated himself on soft red velvet and white fur.

The carriage proceeded along the boulevard; men in rich costumes and tall peaked hats, women in white gowns of many flounces turned to watch.

Ahead lay the State Palace of Sion Trumble. This was a square building at the back of a great garden, the design of which, like the other palaces of Carrai, was at once ornate and pleasantly naive: there were six tall towers encircled by spiral staircases, a dome of glass pentagons held in a web of bronze, terraces with balusters in the shape of nymphs. At a marble ramp the carriage halted; here waited an extremely tall, extremely thin old man in black and gray robes. He carried a mace terminating in an emerald ellipsoid, apparently an insignia of office. He greeted Alusz Iphigenia with measured respect. Baron Thobalt presented him to Gersen: "Uther Caymon, Seneschal of the State Palace."

The seneschal bowed, at the same time casting a critical eye up and down Gersen's stained garments, then flicked his mace. Footmen appeared, escorted Alusz Iphigenia and Gersen into the palace. Across a long salon hung with crystal they walked, on a carpet woven in patterns of lavender, rose, and pale green. They parted in a circular vestibule, each to a side corridor. Gersen was taken to a suite of rooms opening on a walled garden, with blossoming trees surrounding a fountain. After the hardships of the journey, the sudden luxury was unreal.

Gersen bathed in a warm pool, and a barber appeared to shave him. From a wardrobe a valet brought fresh garments: loose dark green trousers gathered at the ankle, a dark blue shirt embroidered in white, green leather slippers with eccentric curled toes, the rakish peaked cap that seemed an essential part of the masculine attire.

In the garden a table had been set with fruit, cakes, and wine. Gersen ate, drank, and wondered why, amid surroundings such as this, Sion Trumble could bring himself to raid corsairs or indulge in any hardships whatever.

He left the apartment and wandered through the palace, finding everywhere furnishings, rugs, and hangings of exquisite craftsmanship: objects of varying styles evidently brought from all the regions of Thamber.

In a drawing room, he came upon the Baron Thobalt who greeted him with somber courtesy. After a moment or two of pondering, Thobalt inquired as to the nature of the outside universe "—from which, so I understand, you have come."

Gersen admitted as much. He described the Oikumene, its various worlds and their organization, the Beyond and its disorganization, the planet Earth from which had issued all humanity. He spoke of Thamber and the legend that it had become, to which the Baron replied that the remainder of humanity was no less a myth to the folk of Thamber. With a trace of melancholy he asked, "No doubt you intend to return to your native environment?"

"In due course," Gersen said cautiously.

"You will then explain that Thamber is after all no myth?"

"I haven't considered the matter," said Gersen. "What is your own feeling? Perhaps you prefer isolation."

Thobalt shook his head. "I am thankful that I need not make this decision. Before today, only a single individual claimed to have visited the worlds of the stars, and this was Kokor Hekkus—but he is denounced everywhere as a hormagaunt—a man without a soul, and not to be trusted."

"You are acquainted with Kokor Hekkus?"

"I have seen him across the field of war."

Gersen forbore to ask if the Baron had noted a similarity with the man Paderbush. Thinking of Paderbush, now a prisoner in the crypts, he felt a twinge of conscience: if the man were not Kokor Hekkus, his only offense was participation in a counter-attack upon the Tadousko-Oi.

Gersen signaled a footman. "Take me to the crypts where my prisoner is confined."

"A moment, Sir Knight, I will inform the seneschal; he alone carries keys to the crypts."

The seneschal presently appeared, considered Gersen's request, then rather grudgingly, or so it seemed, took Gersen to a great door of carved wood, unlocked it to reveal a second iron door, which opened upon a flight of stone steps. These led down a long single flight, into an area paved with granite flags, illuminated by slits communicating with the outside daylight. To one side, iron-barred doors led into cells, only one of which was occupied. The seneschal gestured. "There is your prisoner. If you wish to kill him, be kind enough to use the chamber beyond, where the necessary equipment is at hand."

"I plan nothing like that. I only wanted to assure myself that he suffered nothing ill."

"This is not Aglabat; there is nothing of that sort here."

Gersen went to look through the bars; Paderbush, leaning back in a chair, surveyed him with contemptuous mockery. The cell was dry and airy; on a table were the remnants of an apparently adequate meal.

"You are satisfied?" asked the seneschal.

Gersen turned away with a nod. "A week or two of meditation can do him no great harm. Allow him to see no one but myself."

"As you wish." The seneschal conducted Gersen back to the drawing-room, where now Alusz Iphigenia had joined the Baron. Present were also other ladies and knights of the palace. Alusz Iphigenia looked at Gersen with something like surprise. "I have known you only as a spaceman," she told him. "I am surprised to see you a gentleman of Vadrus."

Gersen grinned. "I haven't changed, in spite of the finery. But you—" he could not find words to express what he wanted to say.

Alusz Iphigenia said rather hurriedly, "I have had word that Sion Trumble returns. He will be with us at this evening's banquet."

Gersen felt an emptiness. He strove to deny it to himself: in spite of his clothes he was no gentleman, of Vadrus or elsewhere; he was Kirth Gersen, survivor of the Mount Pleasant massacre, doomed to a lifetime of dark deeds. He said lightly, "This is what makes you happy—the nearness of your betrothed?"

She shook her head. "He is hardly that, as you well know. I am happy because—but no! I am not happy. I am all at odds with myself!" She gave her hands an excited flutter. "Look! All this is mine, should I want it! I can enjoy all the best of Thamber! But—do I want it? And then there is Kokor Hekkus, who is unpredictable. But somehow I do not think of him. . . . Is it that I prefer the life of a vagabond—that I have seen enough of the worlds beyond Thamber to tantalize me?"

Gersen had nothing to say. She sighed, looked at him from the corner of her eye. "But I have small choice. I am here now and here I must stay. Next week I return to Draszane— and you will be gone. . . . You will, won't you?"

Gersen gave the matter sober thought. "Where and how I go depends on how best I can return to the spaceship."

"And then?"

"And then—I continue with what I came to do."

She sighed. "It seems a bleak prospect. Back to the Skar Sakau. . . . The crags and chasms once more. Then Aglabat. How will you find your way through the walls? And if you are captured—" she grimaced. "When I first heard of the crypts under Aglabat I did not sleep for months; I was afraid to sleep, for fear of the Aglabat crypts."

An attendant in pale green livery passed by with a tray; Alusz Iphigenia took two goblets, gave one to Gersen. "And if you were killed or captured—how could I leave Thamber, if I were of a mind to do so?"

Gersen laughed uncomfortably. "If I thought of these matters, I would fear them. I would be less effective for my fear and hence more likely to suffer capture or death. If you wed Sion Trumble, it appears that you will have the same problems."

Alusz Iphigenia shrugged her slender bare shoulders—she wore the white flounced sleeveless gown characteristic of the city. "He is handsome, gentle, just, gallant—and perhaps too good for me. I suddenly find myself thinking thoughts and wishing wishes I never knew before." She looked around the room, listened a moment to the murmur of conversation, then turned back to Gersen. "I find it hard to express myself—but in a period when men and women fly space almost instantly, when a hundred worlds associate themselves in an Oikumene, when anything seems possible to human reason, this remote little planet with its extremes of virtue and viciousness seems unthinkable."

Gersen, who knew the worlds Beyond and the worlds of the Oikumene much more intimately than Alusz Iphigenia, could not share her feelings. "It depends," he said, "on how you regard humanity: its past, its present, and what you hope for the future. Most people of the Oikumene might agree with you. The Institute—" he laughed hollowly "—probably would prefer more of Thamber in the daily life of the Oikumene."

"I know nothing of the Institute," said Alusz Iphigenia. "Are they evil men, or criminals?"

"No," said Gersen. "They are philosophers. . . ."

Alusz Iphigenia sighed, almost absently, reached forth to take his hand. "There is so much I don't know." A herald marched into the room, followed by pages with long clarions. The herald cried, "Sion Trumble, Grand Prince of Vadrus, enters his palace!"

The room became quiet. A distant measured clanking could be heard in the hall. The pages raised their clarions, blew a fanfare. Into the room strode Sion Trumble, wearing stained armor, a morion dented and smeared with blood. He removed the morion, revealing a mass of blond ringlets, a close-cropped blond beard, a fine straight nose, and the bluest of blue eyes. He raised his arm in salute to all, then marched to Alusz Iphigenia, bowed over her hand. "My princess—you have chosen to return."

Alusz Iphigenia giggled. Sion Trumble looked at her in surprise. "The truth of the matter," said Alusz Iphigenia, "is that this gentleman allowed me no choice."

Sion Trumble turned to inspect Gersen. He and Sion Trumble would never be friends, thought Gersen. Noble, gallant, gentle, and just though Sion Trumble might be, he likewise was almost certainly humorless, self-righteous, and obstinate.

"I have been informed of your coming," Sion Trumble told Gersen. "I noted the dreadful mechanism in which you came. We shall have much to discuss. But now, please excuse me. I go to relieve myself of my armor." He turned, departed the room. The murmur of conversation began again.

Alusz Iphigenia had no more to say, and became almost pensive. An hour later, the company moved to the banquet hall. At an elevated table sat Sion Trumble in robes of scarlet and white flanked by nobles of the realm. Below, ranged other folk in strict order of precedence. Gersen found himself near the outer door, and he noted that Alusz Iphigenia, for all her ostensible standing as the betrothed of Sion Trumble, still gave way to at least six ladies of presumably more elevated rank.

The banquet was long and splendid; the wines were strong. Gersen ate and drank sparingly, answered questions with courtesy, unsuccessfully tried to make himself inconspicuous, for it appeared that every eye was on him.

Sion Trumble ate scantily and drank less. Halfway through the meal he rose, and pleading fatigue, excused himself from the company.

Somewhat later a page came behind Gersen to whisper in his ear: "My lord, at your convenience, the prince wishes to speak with you."

Gersen rose to his feet; the page led him to the circular vestibule, along a corridor, through a door into a small drawing-room paneled in green wood. Here sat Sion Trumble, now wearing a loose gown of pale blue silk. He motioned Gersen to a chair nearby, indicated a tabouret on which stood goblets and flasks. "Be at ease," he said. "You are a man of a far world; please ignore our incomprehensible protocol. We will talk as one man to another, with complete candor. Tell me—why are you here?"

Gersen could see no reason to tell other than the truth. "I came to kill Kokor Hekkus."

Sion Trumble raised his eyebrows. "Alone? How will you storm his walls? How will you defeat the Brown Bersaglers?"

"I don't know."

Sion Trumble looked into the fire that burned in a nearby grate. "As of the moment, truce exists between Misk and Vadrus. There might well have been war when the Princess Iphigenia chose to cast her lot with me, but now it seems that she will have neither of us." He frowned into the fire, gripped the chair handles. "I will provide no provocation."

"Can you help me in any way whatever?" Gersen thought that he might as well learn the worst.

"Conceivably. What is your quarrel with Kokor Hekkus?"

Gersen described the raid on Mount Pleasant. "Five men destroyed my home, killed all my kin, enslaved my friends. I hope to bring retribution to these five. Malagate is dead. Kokor Hekkus will be next."

Sion Trumble frowned and nodded. "You have undertaken what seems a formidable task. Specifically what do you want of me?"

"First, your help and guidance in returning to my space-ship, which I left to the north of the Skar Sakau."

"This I will provide, to the best of my ability. To the north of the Skar are principalities hostile to me, and the Ta-dousko-Oi are implacable."

"There is another aspect to the affair," said Gersen. He hesitated, suddenly aware of another startling possibility that till now he had not recognized. He continued slowly. "When I took the fort from Kokor Hekkus, I took also a prisoner who I thought might be Kokor Hekkus himself. Princess Iphigenia thinks not; but I am uncertain. It seemed unlikely then, and does so now, that Kokor Hekkus could resist the first trial of his new toy. . . . And something about this prisoner reminds me of another man who might also be Kokor Hekkus."

"I can deal with your uncertainty," said Sion Trumble. "In the palace is Baron Erl Castiglianu, once intimately leagued with Kokor Hekkus and now his direst enemy. If anyone will know Kokor Hekkus, the Baron Castiglianu is the man, and tomorrow you may make the test."

"I will be happy to hear his opinion."

Sion Trumble came to a decision. "I cannot help you to any large extent; for I do not visit war or hardship upon my people without good cause. So long as Kokor Hekkus keeps to Aglabat I will not provoke him."

He made a sign: the audience was over. Gersen rose to his feet, left the room. In the antechamber he found the seneschal who conducted him to his apartments. Gersen went out into the garden, looked up at the sky, found the scimitar-shaped cluster: the "God-Boat," and thought of what he must do, and was almost appalled. Yet—what otherwise? Why had he come to Thamber?

He went to bed and slept well. Sunlight streaming into his room awakened him. He bathed, dressed in the most somber of the garments to be found in his wardrobe, ate a breakfast of fruit, pastry, and tea. Clouds rolled in from the west and there was rain in his garden: Gersen watched the drops plash in the pool, and considered the various factors to the situation. Always he returned to the same idea: the identity of Paderbush must be established by one means or another.

A page entered to announce the attendance of Baron Erl Castiglianu. He was a gaunt man of middle-age, stern of demeanor, scarred along both his cheeks. "I have been ordered by Prince Sion Trumble to place my special knowledge at your disposal," he said. "This I shall be pleased to do."

"You are aware of what I require?"

"Not clearly."

"I want you to look closely at a man and tell me whether or not he is Kokor Hekkus."

The baron grimaced. "And what then?"

"You can do this?"

"Assuredly. Notice these scars: they were wrought by the orders of Kokor Hekkus. I hung three days on a rod through my cheeks, living only through hate."

"Come then, let us inspect this man."

"He is here?"

"He is confined below, in the crypts."

The page brought the seneschal, who unlocked the double doors of timber and metal. Into the crypt the three descended. Paderbush stood in the cell, hands on bars, legs apart, staring forth into the outer chamber. Gersen pointed. "This is the man."

The baron advanced, inspected Paderbush closely.

"Well?" asked Gersen.

"No," said the baron after a moment. "This is not Kokor Hekkus. At least—no, I am sure not. . . . Although the eyes look at me with evil wisdom. . . . No, He is a stranger. I have never met him at Aglabat or elsewhere."

"Very well then, it appears I have been wrong." Gersen turned to the seneschal. "Open the door."

"You intend to release the man?"

"Not completely. But he need no longer be confined in a dungeon."

The seneschal unlocked the door. "Come forth," said Gersen. "It appears that I have done you an injustice."

Paderbush slowly stepped from the cell; he had not been expecting release, and he moved warily.

Gersen took him by the wrist, using a grip that could instantly be transposed into an arm-lock. "Come along; back up the stairs."

"Where do you take this man?" the seneschal inquired petulantly.

"Prince Sion Trumble and I will jointly make a decision," said Gersen. To Baron Erl Castiglianu he said: "My thanks for your cooperation; you have been helpful."

Baron Castiglianu hesitated. "This man may be a villain in any case; he may seek to overpower you."

Gersen displayed the projac he carried in his left hand. "I am prepared for anything."

The baron bowed, walked swiftly away, relieved to be discharged of his obligation. Gersen took Paderbush to his apartments, closed the door upon the seneschal.

Gersen seated himself in a leisurely manner; Paderbush stood in the center of the room and finally asked: "What do you plan with me now?"

"I am still puzzled," said Gersen. "Possibly you are the man you say you are; in which case I know nothing of your discredit, other than the fact that you serve Kokor Hekkus. Still, I would not have you pent in a dungeon for hypothetical crimes. You are soiled, will you bathe?"

"No."

"You prefer sweat and grime? Perhaps you would change your clothes?"

"No."

Gersen shrugged. "As you wish."

Paderbush folded his arms, glared down at Gersen. "Why do you restrain me here?"

Gersen considered, "I suspect that your life is in danger. I mean to protect you."

"I am well able to protect myself."

"Nevertheless, please seat yourself in that chair yonder." Gersen pointed with the tip of his projac. "You stand like a wild beast about to pounce, and this makes me uneasy."

Paderbush gave him a cold grin, seated himself. "I have done you no harm," he said presently. "But you have humiliated me, thrown me into a dungeon, and now you ply me with hints and innuendos. I tell you, Kokor Kekkus is not a man to overlook purposeful wrongs done to his underlings. If you wish to spare your host much embarrassment I suggest that you discharge me from custody, that I may return to Aglabat."

"You know Kokor Hekkus well?" Gersen asked in a tone of easy conversation.

"Certainly. He is a man like a Khasferug eagle. His eyes glitter with intelligence. His joy and his anger are both like fire, and sweep all before them. His imagination is as broad as the sky; everyone wonders regarding the thoughts that form and pass behind his brow, and from what source they are derived."

"Interesting," said Gersen. "I am eager to meet him—as I shall soon do."

Paderbush was incredulous. "You are to meet Kokor Hekkus?"

Gersen nodded. "You and I will return to Aglabat in the fort—after a week or two of rest here at Carrai."

"I prefer to leave at this moment."

"Impossible. I want no notice of my arrival; I wish to surprise Kokor Hekkus."

Paderbush sneered. "You are a fool. You are more than a fool. How can you surprise Kokor Hekkus? He knows more of your movements than you do yourself."

CHAPTER 12

From "The Avatar's Apprentice," in *Scroll from the Ninth Dimension:*

There was no cessation to the haze that extended right and left in gelid layers, and up was as good as down. There was a sense of comings and goings, of invisible fluttering messages: all quite beyond Marmaduke's apprehension. He began to suspect that somehow the Doctrine of Temporal Stasis had effected a transposition of percepts. Why else, he wondered, as he groped through the mauve suffusion, should the word 'lachrymose' occur to him again and again and again?

He found himself at the edge of a bulging limpid window, beyond which danced anamorphotic visions. Looking up he spied a fringe of curving rods; below he found a pink curving shelf,. in which were embedded more of these rods. To the side a lumpy porous object thrust forth like a prodigious nose: and he now saw the object to be a nose in all verity, a most extraordinary object. Marmaduke altered the trend of his musings. The central problem, so it seemed, was to learn from whose eye he looked forth. Much, after all, would depend upon his viewpoint.

The morning passed. Paderbush at times seemed to doze in the chair, at times seemed vividly alert, on the verge of a sudden attack upon Gersen. After one of these tense periods Gersen said, "I urge you to patience. First, as you know, I carry a weapon—" he held the projac up into Paderbush's view "—and second, even without it you could do nothing against me."

"Are you so sure?" Paderbush asked with weary insolence. "We are of a size; let us try a fall or two, and see who is the better man."

"Thank you; not on this occasion. Why should we exert ourselves? Presently we will have our noon meal, so let us relax."

"As you wish."

At the door sounded a tap-tap-tap. Gersen went to stand by the thick panel. "Who is there?"

"It is Uther Caymon, seneschal," came the muffled voice. "Open the door, if you please."

Gersen did so; the seneschal stepped forward. "The Prince wishes to see you in his chambers at once. He has heard the opinion of the Baron Erl Castiglianu and he begs that the prisoner be given his freedom; he wishes to provide Kokor Hekkus no pretext for contentiousness."

"I definitely intend to relinquish all control over this man, in due course," said Gersen. "But now he has agreed to accept the hospitality of Sion Trumble for possibly two weeks."

"That is generous of him," observed the seneschal drily, "inasmuch as the Grand Prince has been so remiss as to forget to proffer this same hospitality. Will you accompany me to the apartments of Prince Sion Trumble?"

Gersen rose to his feet. "With pleasure. What will I do with our guest? I dare not leave him, nor do I care to go everywhere arm in arm with him."

"Return him to the dungeon," said the seneschal crossly. "This is hospitality adequate for his sort."

"The Grand Prince would not agree to this," declared Gersen. "He has only just requested that I release the man."

The seneschal blinked. "That is so."

"Please convey my apologies, and ask if he will condescend to meet me here."

The seneschal made a gruff noise, threw up his hands in a helpless gesture, threw a baleful side-glance toward Paderbush and left the room.

Gersen and Paderbush sat facing each other. "Tell me," said Gersen, "are you acquainted with a man named Seuman Otwal?"

"I have heard his name mentioned."

"He is an associate of Kokor Hekkus. You and he have certain mannerisms in common."

"That may well be true—perhaps because of our association with Kokor Hekkus. . . . What are these mannerisms?"

"An attitude of the head, a certain set of gesticulations, what I might call a psychic aura. Very strange indeed."

Paderbush nodded solemnly, but said no more. A few minutes later Alusz Iphigenia came to the door, and was admitted. She glanced in surprise from Gersen to Paderbush. "Why is this man here?"

"He thinks the solitude of the dungeon unjust, since his offenses number only a dozen or so murders."

Paderbush grinned wolfishly. "I am Paderbush, Knight Junior of Castle Pader; none of my line have shunned taking a life or two, at the risk of his own."

Alusz Iphigenia turned away, addressed herself to Gersen. "Carrai is not so gay as before. Something has changed, something is lacking: perhaps it is in me. . . . I want to return to Draszane, to my home."

"I thought that a great gala was being planned in your honor."

Alusz Iphigenia shrugged. "Perhaps it has already been forgotten. Sion Trumble is angry with me—or at least is not so gallant as before." She gave Gersen a quick side-glance. "Perhaps he is jealous."

" 'Jealous?' Why should he be jealous?"

"After all, you and I spent much time alone. This is enough to arouse suspicion—and jealousy."

"Ridiculous," said Gersen.

Alusz Iphigenia raised her eyebrows. "Am I so ill-favored? Is the mere suggestion of such a relationship so absurd?"

"Not at all," said Gersen. "To the contrary. But we must not let Sion Trumble suffer such a misconception." He summoned a page, sent him to request audience with Sion Trumble.

The page presently returned, to announce that the prince was seeing no one.

"Return," said Gersen. "Convey to Sion Trumble this message. say that tomorrow I must depart. If necessary I will ride the fort north of the Skar Sakau and somehow find my spaceship. Also, inform the prince that Princess Iphigenia plans to accompany me. Inquire now if he will see us."

Alusz Iphigenia turned to Gersen. "You really mean to take me?"

"If you care to return to the Oikumene."

"But what of Kokor Hekkus? I thought—"

"A detail."

"Then you're not serious," said Alusz Iphigenia sadly.

"Yes. Will you come with me?"

She hesitated, then nodded. "Yes. Why not? Your life is real. My life—all of Thamber—none of it is real. It is animated myth, archaic scenes from a diorama. It stifles me."

"Very well. We will leave very soon."

Alusz Iphigenia looked at Paderbush. "What of him?" she

asked dubiously. "Will you free him, or leave him for Sion Trumble?"

"No. He comes with us."

Alusz Iphigenia turned a puzzled glance at Gersen. "With—us?"

"Yes. For a brief period."

Paderbush rose to his feet, stretched his arms. "This conversation bores me. I will never go with you."

"Oh? Not even so far as Aglabat, to meet Kokor Hekkus?"

"I go to Aglabat alone—and now." He sprang through the apartment, fled across the garden, bounded up and over the wall. He was gone.

Alusz Iphigenia ran to look across the garden, then turned to Gersen. "Call the attendants! He can't get far, these gardens are all part of the inner courtyard. Hurry!"

Gersen seemed in no desperate haste. Alusz Iphigenia tugged at his arm. "Do you wish him to escape?"

"No," said Gersen, with sudden energy. "He must not escape. We will inform Sion Trumble, who will best know how to recapture him. Come."

In the corridor Gersen ordered the page, "Take us quickly to Sion Trumble's apartments; on the run!"

The page led them along a corridor, to the circular vestibule, down another red-carpeted hall to a broad white door. Here stood two guards in white uniforms with black iron morions.

"Open!" said Gersen. "We must see Sion Trumble at once."

"No, my lord. We have orders from the seneschal to admit no one."

Gersen aimed his projac at the lock. There was a blaze of fire and smoke; the guards cried out in protest. Gersen said, "Stand back, guard the hall; for the safety of Vadrus!"

The guards hesitated, half-dazed. Gersen thrust open the door, entered with Alusz Iphigenia.

They stood in an entry, with white marble statues looking down from alcoves. Gersen peered along one hall, through an archway, walked up to a closed door, listened. From beyond came the sound of movement. He tried the door: it was locked. He used his projac, burst the door open, charged into the room.

Sion Trumble, half-clad, leapt around in startlement. He opened his mouth, bawled something incomprehensible. Alusz Iphigenia gasped: "He's wearing the clothes of Paderbush!"

This was true: on a frame hung Sion Trumble's green and blue robes; he had been divesting the stained garments worn by Paderbush. Now he reached for his sword; Gersen hacked at his wrist, struck it from his hand. Sion Trumble reached to a shelf where reposed a hand-weapon; Gersen destroyed it with a blast of his projac.

Sion Trumble turned slowly, sprang at Gersen like a wild beast. Gersen laughed aloud, stooped, caught his shoulder in Sion Trumble's belly, grabbed the instantly raised knee, tossed him through the air. He caught at the blond curly hair, and as Sion Trumble struggled and surged, pulled. Off came the blond hair, off came the entire face, leaving Gersen holding a warm rubbery sac by the hair, the fine straight nose tilted askew, the mouth lolled open. The man on the floor had no face. The scalp, the face muscles showed pink and red through a film of transparent tissue. The eyes glared lidless under a bare forehead, above a black nostril gap. The lipless mouth grimaced, white with its suddenly conspicuous teeth.

"Who—what is *that?*" asked Alusz Iphigenia in a hushed voice.

"That," said Gersen, "is a hormagaunt. It is Kokor Hekkus. Or Billy Windle. Or Seuman Otwal. Or Paderbush. Or a dozen others. And now his time has come. Kokor Hekkus—recall the raid on Mount Pleasant? I have come to bring you retribution."

Kokor Hekkus rose slowly to his feet, death's head of a face staring.

"Once you told me that you feared only death," said Gersen. "Now you are to die."

Kokor Hekkus made a gasping sound.

Gersen said, "You have lived the most evil of lives. I should kill you with the utmost terror and pain—but it is sufficient that you die." He pointed his projac. Kokor Hekkus gave a wild hoarse sound, flung forward with arms and legs wide, to be met by a gush of fire.

The following day Seneschal Uther Caymon was hanged at the public gallows: the accessory, creature, companion, and confidant of Kokor Hekkus. Standing on a tall jointed ladder he yelled down to the awed crowd, "Fools! Fools! Do you realize how long you have been gulled and milked, and bled? Of your gold, of your warriors, of your beautiful women? For two hundred years! I am this old, Kokor Hekkus was older! Against the Brown Bersaglers he sent your best and they died in futility; to his bed came your beautiful girls; some returned to their homes, others did not. You will cry when you hear of how they fared! At last he died, at last I die, but fools! fools!—"

The executioner had broken the ladder. The crowd stared hollow-eyed at the jerking figure.

Alusz Iphigenia and Gersen walked in the garden at the palace of Baron Endel Thobalt. She still was pale with horror. "How did you know? You knew—but how?"

"First I suspected from Sion Trumble's hands. He had the wit to carry himself differently from Paderbush, but his hands were the same: long-fingered, a smooth glossy skin, thin thumbs with long nails. I saw these hands, but was deceived—until once more I saw Paderbush at close range. Sion Trumble disclosed himself further. He was aware that you had decided not to wed him: he told me so. But only three people knew: you, me, and Paderbush, for only in the fort did you make up your mind. When I heard Sion Trumble make this statement then I looked at his hands, and I knew."

"What an evil thing. I wonder what planet bore him, who were his parents. . . ."

"He was a man blessed and cursed with his imagination. A single life was insufficient for him; he must drink at every spring, know every experience, live to all extremes. On Thamber he found a world to his temperament. In his various entities he created his own epics. When he tired of Thamber, he returned to the other worlds of man—less amenable to his will, but nonetheless amusing. He is dead."

"And now more than ever I must leave Thamber," said Alusz Iphigenia.

"There is nothing to keep us. Tomorrow we shall leave."

"Why tomorrow? Let us leave now. I think—I am sure— that I can take us to the spaceship. The way north around the Skar is not hard; the landmarks are known."

"There is no need to stay," said Gersen. "Let us go."

A small group of Carrai noblemen gathered in the late afternoon light. Baron Endel Thobalt spoke with sudden anxiety: "You will send back ships from the Oikumene?"

Gersen nodded. "I have agreed to do so, and I will."

Alusz Iphigenia, heaving a small sigh, looked around the

landscape. "Someday—I don't know when—I will come back to Thamber too."

"Remember," Gersen told the baron, "that if ships from the Oikumene arrive your old ways will not last! There will be grumbling and nostalgia and dissatisfaction. Perhaps you prefer Thamber as it is now?"

"I can speak only for myself," said Endel Thobalt. "I say that we must rejoin humanity, no matter what the cost."

He was echoed by his fellows.

"As you wish," said Gersen. Alusz Iphigenia climbed within, Gersen followed, clamped the hatch, went to the console, looked down at the bronze plaque:

Patch Engineering and Construction Company
Patris, Krokinole

"Good ole Patch," said Gersen. "I'll have to send him a report on how his machine worked—presuming that it carries us back to the spaceship."

Alusz Iphigenia, standing beside him, pressed her head lightly against his shoulder. Looking down into the shining dusty-golden hair, Gersen remembered how first he had seen her at Interchange, how first he had thought her unremarkable. He laughed quietly. Alusz Iphigenia looked up. "Why do you laugh?"

"Someday you'll know. But not right now."

Smiling at some private recollection of her own, Alusz Iphigenia said no more.

Gersen thrust the GO lever ahead. Thirty-six legs rose and fell; eighteen segments moved forward. The fort slid off to the north-west, where the long light of the afternoon sun glinted on the white peaks of the Skar Sakau.

A GALAXY OF SCIENCE FICTION STARS!

LEE CORREY Manna	UE1896—$2.95
TIMOTHY ZAHN The Blackcollar	UE1843—$2.95
A.E. VAN VOGT Computerworld	UE1879—$2.50
COLIN KAPP Search for the Sun	UE1858—$2.25
ROBERT TREBOR An XT Called Stanley	UE1865—$2.50
ANDRE NORTON Horn Crown	UE1635—$2.95
JACK VANCE The Face	UE1921—$2.50
E.C. TUBB Angado	UE1908—$2.50
KENNETH BULMER The Diamond Contessa	UE1853—$2.50
ROGER ZELAZNY Deus Irae	UE1887—$2.50
PHILIP K. DICK Ubik	UE1859—$2.50
DAVID J. LAKE Warlords of Xuma	UE1832—$2.50
CLIFFORD D. SIMAK Our Children's Children	UE1880—$2.50
M.A. FOSTER Transformer	UE1814—$2.50
GORDON R. DICKSON Mutants	UE1809—$2.95
BRIAN STABLEFORD The Gates of Eden	UE1801—$2.50
JOHN BRUNNER The Jagged Orbit	UE1917—$2.95
EDWARD LLEWELLYN Salvage and Destroy	UE1898—$2.95
PHILIP WYLIE The End of the Dream	UE1900—$2.25

Buy them at your local bookstore or use this convenient coupon for ordering.

NEW AMERICAN LIBRARY,
P.O. Box 999, Bergenfield, New Jersey 07621

Please send me the DAW BOOKS I have checked above. I am enclosing
$——————— (check or money order—no currency or C.O.D.'s). Please
include the list price plus $1.00 per order to cover handling costs.

Name ————————————————————————————

Address ——————————————————————————

City ———————————— State ————— Zip Code————————
Please allow at least 4 weeks for delivery